A JOURNEY FOR ROWNA THE LONER

Humble Beginnings vs. Glamorous Endings

By

SHERENE WHYTE

DEDICATION

I dedicate this book to my gorgeous children Keisha, Kareem, Joshua and Samuel, my mother Lorna and a dear friend Mr George Brown.

CONTENTS

ACKNOWLEDGMENTS

The memories of my great aunt Vivienne McFarlane (now deceased) remain with me to this very day and I hold those values that she instilled in me as a child, which have guided me through life, very dear to my heart. Her presence is no longer here with us but I sometimes hear her voice in my own mind repeating her parables and find myself using the very same to my own children. I also give thanks to the most high God.

Rowna was born in Jamaica and cared for by her Grandma Pearle which is a regular occurrence in the traditional Jamaican family. Grandparents are highly respected and are the backbone of many families. They are very active in helping to raise their grandchildren and have a lot of influence in making important decisions regarding their wellbeing and upbringing.

In my own experience my grandmother's involvement in my life as a child was significant and I appreciated her input in many ways. When grandparents eventually die the funerals are indeed quite sorrowful because they were expected to be around forever by their grandchildren.

The sad part of losing a grandparent usually is the fact that when all their hard work materialises in their grandchildren, they are unable to reap any benefits as they are usually deceased. For Rowna her grandmother was one in a million and though she was old fashioned in her beliefs, she was a woman of valour and integrity. Grandma Pearle's drive to release her granddaughter from a poverty-stricken life proved its worth in the end.

Many Jamaicans would say Rowna's outcome made Grandma Pearle smile in her grave!

Chapter 1

Introduction

Rowna lived in a small house, near the gully side in Kingston, Jamaica. She was not much of a talker and kept very much to herself; instead she enjoyed her own company which allowed her to daydream about her aspirations and the places she was going to visit when she reached adulthood.

Rowna knew that her purpose in life would lead her to be somebody of importance but she just did not realise how true that was until her mission was accomplished. She came from a poor background and at times did not know whether she would have sufficient meals to eat daily. However, her grandmother was so proud that even if they did not have food to cook on a daily basis she would light firewood and put a pot of water with herbs such as thyme and a clove of garlic on the stove to boil so that when the nosey neighbours would peek through the holes in the zinc fence, they would be convinced that she was preparing the evening meal and had nothing to gossip about. The neighbours were of poor background themselves but had relatives abroad who sent foreign goods in barrels for them yearly, and so they would show off by cooking up a storm every evening, preparing their meals with sweet-scented aromas from the salt fish with ackee and tuna with rice, not to forget the Sunday rice and peas and chicken.

Rowna tried very hard to achieve good grades in school and she sure wasn't a dunce. Each morning before Rowna went to school she had to get her daily chores done. She first fetched water from the cistern across the road from where she lived; then she swept the leaves that fell from the trees overnight and animal droppings from the yard. She picked fresh mint from the mint plant her grandmother grew in the front garden and boiled tea for both of them. She strained the tea using a net cloth and put her grandmother's portion in a medium-sized thermos so she would have enough herbal tea to last her for the day. If any hard dough bread was left over from the previous day she would butter two slices or prepare some cornmeal porridge to have with her tea.

Rowna would then get ready for school and start her journey after waving goodbye to Grandma Pearle who would stand by the gate making sure that her granddaughter was safe especially in the later months of the year; the mornings were dark and the community where Rowna lived was not always safe, in fact some people called it 'No Man's Land'. It was so called because people would disappear out of thin air when they walked through there, especially at night, and it was better to mind your own business than to meddle and disappear yourself if seen as one that could not mind their own business. Once Rowna went out of sight, Grandma Pearle would head back in to start her day, getting the washing done early and putting it out to dry on the clothesline before midday.

Rowna lived some distance from school and so she had to get a JOS (Jamaica Omnibus Service) bus to school, or if the bus was full then in order to get to school on time she would hop on a minivan which costed a bit more but there was not a lot of choice so it was either that or walk. Sometimes the conductor on the minibus would try to put inappropriate argument to Rowna because she was beautiful and was of brown complexion, however, she didn't take much notice of that type of behaviour, instead she just smiled and said nothing as all she was interested in was getting to school.

Rowna used to pray hard that she would not have to travel with Loudmouth Lucy who would from the bottom of the road, shout, "Rowna, wait for me!" When Lucy had a conversation with anyone she would do most of the talking and everyone within a mile radius could hear what she was discussing. She was a true 'brawl'. The trick was to forget the bus and jump on the nearest minivan when you heard her calling hoping that she would not be able to get on. Lucy knew everyone and she chatted a lot, so no one told her their secrets because they wouldn't be secret anymore. As a matter of fact, JBC (Jamaica Broadcasting Corporation) was not a challenge for her because she could spread news faster than any media.

When Lucy finally met Rowna in the playground or on her lunch break, she would ask, "Didn't you hear me calling you this morning?"

To be honest it is only the deaf would not have heard her, but to be polite Rowna would reply, "No, you sure it was me you saw this morning?" It was hard to get away from her unless you told some kind of lie and luckily most of the time it worked, even though at times Rowna knew she had her doubts.

Rowna attended Tivoli Garden Comprehensive High School morning classes. There were two shifts, morning and evening. The morning shift started at 7:30am and the evening shift at 1:00pm. Rowna would have preferred attending a different school but as they were poor they had to settle for affordability. Tivoli Garden Comprehensive High was in Kingston and it was a very good, no-nonsense school. The teachers were quite strict and uniforms and appearance were checked routinely to ensure the school's dress codes were met. If you turned up at school without your school tie or incorrect uniform then you would be sent back home, so the students who attended had to follow protocol or attend another school. This helped Rowna to be a disciplined adult; this was to be proven relevant and helpful to her chosen career path.

Rowna was left with her grandparents to raise her when her mother (Annette) left for the United States to seek employment and improve her life. However, Annette though she promised her parents that she would file for Rowna to join her, once she had settled, failed to keep her promise and so Rowna was abandoned and left to the mercy of her grandparents. Rowna's grandfather was heartbroken when his daughter left and never looked back as she was the apple of his eyes and he spoiled her without reservations. Grandpa Brim bragged about his daughter to all the neighbours and though Grandma Pearle always warned him about spoiling her and failing to scold her when her behaviour warranted such actions, he would laugh and say that she was only a child and would eventually grow out of it.

Grandpa Brim died shortly after Rowna's mum migrated and so her grandmother had full responsibility to take care of her. Grandma Pearle loved Rowna very much but as she was only a pensioner with very little income they had to make do with what they had available to them. Grandma Pearle was a proud woman who never asked for help unless absolutely necessary. She did not rely on the extended family for financial help because she claimed that asking for help was another term for begging and she prided herself in regularly proclaiming that she was 'no beggar'. She lived by her means and instead of complaining about what she did not have, she gave thanks to God for what she possessed. Rowna's grandma was particularly aware of her surroundings and hated gossiping, so she did not mingle too much and had little to say; most of the time she only said good morning and good evening to her neighbours and Rowna felt that the only reason she did that was because one of her regular proverbs was 'manners maketh a man', so in order to honour this proverb and not be seen as a hypocrite she had no choice but to greet her neighbours when she saw them.

They lived in a small two-bedroom house that was not adequately maintained but they were comfortable and happy in it. Rowna was not allowed visitors without her grandmother's permission and she said that Rowna did not have time for friends as she needed her spare time for studies and her philosophy was that friends were not important and can only bring trouble so your guess is as good as mine; poor Rowna had no friends visiting unless they were vetted and scrutinised by Grandma Pearle, which was virtually an impossible test to pass.

According to Nadine, one of the neighbours' daughter who was the same age as Rowna, she told her that it was rumoured that Grandma Pearle's best friend Miss Carmen did a real dirty when she stole her boyfriend (Jerry) whom she was dating for five years. They had met in high school and had plans to get married and start a life of their own together but the crafty Carmen sneakily lowered Jerry and weaved him into her net by persuading Jerry to visit her at home as she was planning a surprise birthday party for Pearle. When Jerry arrived she made cocktails and spiked it with 100% full proof Jamaican white rum, so as they spoke about this imaginary party that Carmen had no intention of throwing for her friend, Jerry got drunk and Carmen took advantage of him under duress so fell pregnant for Jerry.

Jerry did not marry Carmen as she so intended but Pearle, learning about this as Carmen made it known that Jerry was the father of her unborn child in an argument between them, ended the relationship with him. Pearle was heartbroken and so was Jerry as he really loved Pearle. Three years later Jerry was shot and killed in a gang shootout after migrating to the USA with his parents before the child was born. This Rowna felt was the main reason why Grandma Pearle did not like friends as such and so she felt that not allowing her granddaughter to associate with and keep friends would help protect her from what she had endured in her young life.

Rowna used her time wisely; she read books to pass time and she studied hard as she had very little disturbance. Her grandmother's intention was not bad, but Rowna's social skills were underdeveloped as she did not have much freedom to practice in this area. Grandma Pearle had plans for Rowna when she finished High School; she was going to ask her nephew Neville to help her granddaughter to attend university (Stats) so she could graduate and be 'somebody'. Grandma Pearle had already discussed this with her nephew who had agreed provided that Rowna got good grades in the sixth form.

Chapter 2

Rowna Meets Her Fellow

"**R**owna, you are now a woman who can have babies so stay away from boys," warned Grandma Pearle. Rowna had just had her first period and so this was the way folks of Grandma Pearle's age would explain 'sex' to young girls. The good news is that sex education is taught in school so children were not completely ignorant of where babies came from. Rowna tried desperately to avoid the opposite sex's gestures. She was attractive and so boys were naturally drawn to her, but Rowna did not encourage their advances in any way. This was to last for a time only as Jeff Pritchard was certainly not going to give up on his pursuit to secure a relationship with Rowna. He was happy just to seek friendship first but he intended to take that friendship to higher heights later.

Jeff was 6 feet 5 inches tall and had a pale complexion; his mother was of Maroon heritage and his father of Chinese origin. Jeff was a well sought-after young chap who could have his pick of the choice of girls as he was well known for sports such as cricket and football. Girls from every year from 7th grade to 13th grade had their eyes on him, however, he was not interested in the girls who were interested in him; instead he was drawn to the one that showed no interest. He preferred to do the chasing, so when he caught his prey he would feel he was a conqueror.

Jeff attended the same school as Rowna and he could not help but take notice of her in class. She was much disciplined, never getting into trouble, sat on her own mostly and was very quiet. He felt that she would make a trophy girlfriend. Jeff himself was well known throughout the school as he took part in football, being one of the school's best. Jeff was friends with Lucy; yes, 'Loudmouth Lucy'. The only way he could communicate with Rowna, he knew was through Lucy. He arranged with Lucy to go to lunch with him and invite Rowna; as usual she tried to escape but Lucy wasn't taking no for an answer this time. Rowna agreed to have lunch with Lucy as she offered to pay and whilst they were having lunch in the canteen Jeff sneakily joined and behaved as though it was not arranged.

Though Grandma Pearle did not want Rowna to keep friends at home, Rowna had to communicate with others in her class, but she did not find it easy to bond with any particular person especially as she could not invite them home, plus it was embarrassing having to explain to people. She figured out that even if friends accepted this situation for a while then they would get fed up of her as she was not allowed to visit their homes either. The alternative to that was just being a loner, that way there was no one to explain such a ridiculous situation to. The good thing about Lucy, in a way, is that she asked no questions about Rowna's background and she was persistent in being a friend whether Rowna wanted to be her friend or not. In a reassuring way this was good for Rowna because had Lucy not been that way inclined then she surely would be friendless.

Rowna for the first time sat with a boy for lunch, though it was a threesome, but she had no idea about the plan and so wasn't worried. However, Rowna was sure to be careful as she could hear Grandma Pearle's warning in her head: "Stay away from boys." Jeff spoke about his siblings and his family life, which sounded astonishing and breath-taking. He told her that he travelled in the summer holidays to China and USA alternately. Jeff's life sounded exciting to Rowna and indeed sounded more like a fairytale to her as she had never been on an aeroplane or even a boat for that matter. Jeff's cologne smelt lovely and he had piercing bright eyes. At the end of lunch time they bade each other goodbye and went off to their separate lessons. Well! Jeff had managed to "break the ice", he had gotten a foot in. The next day at school Jeff said hello to Rowna, who casually said hello in reply. This went on for a few weeks and finally Rowna became friends with Jeff and they had lunch together regularly since Jeff paid most times. Jeff invited her to watch him play football and cricket matches in school and they developed a close relationship as friends. Grandma Pearle began to notice several changes in her granddaughter; she was getting home later than usual after school and asking to attend after-school activities such as netball. Grandma Pearle may have been old but she certainly was no fool.

"Rowna, where yuh coming from at this hour of the day?" asked Grandma Pearle. Without waiting for a response she said, "Yuh turn big woman now, going in and out as you please."

She then paused and Rowna, shaking in her shoes replied, "I was at netball, Grandma; remember I told you this morning."

Grandma Pearle shook her head with a disappointed look on her face and said to Rowna, "Well I have warned you and so when trouble come, yuh better have your plans ready as to where you going to live, because there is no room here for extras." Grandma Pearle was very serious about what she said and Rowna knew just that.

Two years had passed and by now the relationship with

Jeff had gotten serious and he was now Rowna's other half. Jeff wanted to take the relationship to another level as Rowna was 17 years old and he was 18. He invited Rowna to visit his parents and they accepted Rowna as a daughter, but both you and I know that Rowna could not do the same with Jeff because Grandma Pearle had no intention of meeting him and she was unwilling to even acknowledge that he existed. Rowna was very sad about this as she loved Grandma Pearle very much, plus she knew that she was her surrogate mother now as her own mother had deserted them both.

Rowna continued to see Jeff in secret but cunning Grandma Pearle was about to call in her favour with her nephew Neville because as expected, Rowna got excellent grades in her 'A levels' and was now going on to university.

The neighbour's daughter Nadine, branded as a troublemaker by the community, started to spread rumours about Rowna. Nadine's best friend Emily attended the same school as Rowna and since Jeff was the most popular boy of the school many girls envied her especially because she did not share details of her relationship with any of them and kept very much to herself. Emily told Nadine that Rowna was in a relationship and so word got round and got back to Aunt Pearle's ears.

Chapter 3

Rowna Leaves for University

Well the day finally arrived when Uncle Neville came to visit and the plan was for Rowna to go back with him to Spanish Town where he resided and attend university (UWI) whilst living with him and his family. She would help out with looking after their children and doing the housework in exchange for her fees for university and her upkeep. Things went as planned; Jeff and Rowna said their goodbyes with the intention of seeing each other at intervals as Jeff was also going to start an apprenticeship in Montego Bay so they would only be able to see each other in their holidays.

Uncle Neville stayed only for one week as he had to get back for work and Rowna returned with him. She loved her new home and the family was lovely. Uncle Neville and Aunt Vivian (his wife) had two children who were aged five and seven. They were at primary school and as Rowna only attended university three days per week she was able to help out with the daily chores and things ran smoothly, at least for a while. The children loved Rowna a whole lot and they followed her around constantly when she was at home with them because she showed them kindness and always spent the time playing with them and telling fables. Miranda, the five-year-old, refused to go to bed at nights until Rowna bathed her and read her a bedtime story.

As planned Rowna visited her grandmother in the holidays and at that time Jeff would visit his parents also, so she and Jeff would see each other then. In time Jeff got to meet Grandma Pearle, though reluctantly, but Rowna did not get pregnant as Grandma Pearle assumed she would; she felt at least they were careful and made sensible decisions. Grandma's speciality was cooking fried chicken with rice and peas on a Sunday, and Rowna was sure to eat as much as she could as the meal was 'finger-licking good' and it was her favourite dish.

One night when Rowna had retired to bed, the lights were out and she was dozing off, she heard footsteps in the hallway, then her bedroom door slowly opened giving the impression that whoever it was desperately tried not to make any noticeable sound. Rowna pretended to be in a deep sleep because she felt it may have been a burglar who had broken in, so he would take what he wanted and leave her unharmed provided he believed she didn't see him and she was fast asleep. After lying completely still for some minutes, she felt a hand moving the sheets from her lower part of her body; she quivered and then felt a hand over her mouth, pressing against her lips tightly. She grabbed the hand that covered her mouth and tried to scream but his grasp was so tight and his arms so powerful that she heard no sound. She then turned to see who it was; he looked at her with a wide sneer and put his finger by his lips, implying that she should be quiet.

To her surprise it was her Uncle Neville; though she tried to push him away he got closer and closer. He whispered to Rowna, "You are very attractive and have a hot body; I am in love with you and hope you feel the same about me, darling." Rowna could not scream or call out to his wife who was in the room down the hallway. Uncle Neville ripped her night dress off whilst she struggled trying to stop him and stripped her naked, he then penetrated her young body, thrusting himself inside of her mercilessly. When he finished having his wicked way, he threatened her, saying he would deny anything she said and that if she told his wife what had happen he would make her life a misery and she would not be able to complete university as he would stop paying her fees.

Poor Rowna did not know what to do; if she told his wife he was sure to put her out and if she told her grandmother she would probably die of heartbreak. She thought of telling Jeff but feared that he may take drastic measures towards the uncle that could land him in prison. Rowna was cornered and all seemed hopeless. She needed to finish her degree, so that she could pursue a career and help her grandmother who had sacrificed so much for her to get to this level in life. Rowna comforted herself in believing that one day in the future justice would be served to Neville and she was going to make sure of that.

For the next year and a half Rowna was subject to Uncle Neville's abuse; she saw no way out. It was the summer of 1981 when finally Rowna graduated from University Stats. She returned home to live with Grandma Pearle who was now quite frail and needed to be cared for. Rowna found a job in a local supermarket as jobs were difficult to find. Grandma Pearle had had two strokes whilst Rowna was away at university but she recovered, however due to her age she was not as able bodied as she was in the past. Rowna completed her degree in Criminology (Law) and decided to go on to teaching but though she had applied for several positions she was unsuccessful in securing a job. A friend of Jeff's parents offered Rowna a job as a cashier in their local supermarket. She worked part-time which allowed her to take care of her grandmother for a few years until she passed away. Jeff and Rowna were still together after they both finished their studies and training. Jeff was now a qualified plumber and managed to secure a full-time job close by.

The marriage took place at a registry office as they had little funds left in their savings account. The wedding was done on a small scale as Rowna had very few family members; the guests mainly consisted of Jeff's family and friends.

Shortly after Jeff and Rowna got married he moved in with Grandma Pearle and Rowna. It was but a short time after the move that Rowna began to suspect that Jeff was up to no good because his mobile phone would ring at times and he would suddenly announce that he had to go out due to various given reasons. Some of them made no sense to Rowna. Grandma Pearle warned Rowna to be vigilant and careful because she could sense that Jeff was up to his tricks, but as we all know Grandma was not a great fan of Jeff, so Rowna did not take her warning seriously. Grandma Pearle began to talk about documents regarding the house to be left to Rowna and where the paperwork was kept. She also made it very clear to Rowna the type of funeral service she expected and the pastor she wanted to conduct the service. She told her that she wanted to be buried and not cremated and her resting place was already chosen. Rowna found this disturbing but she knew that she was relied upon by her grandmother to make the arrangements for her funeral. Rowna took excellent care of Grandma Pearle until she drew her last breath that peaceful night in April in the comfort of her own bed.

One morning before Rowna left for work she went to check on her grandma as usual but when she called her she got no response. She then went to nudge her on the shoulder but still she did not move. Rowna noticed that she felt cold and when she investigated further she realised that Grandma Pearle must have died in the night, peacefully whilst sleeping. She called the neighbours which is the usual thing to do in Jamaica, who comforted Rowna until her doctor was notified and came to certify her body deceased, and then got the mortuary to remove the body. Rowna made funeral arrangements for Grandma Pearle after shedding many tears, with the help of her husband, Jeff, and she was buried at Calvary Cemetery in Kingston exactly as she instructed her granddaughter.

Chapter 4

Jeff Gets Caught

Two years after Grandma Pearl died Rowna gave birth to a handsome baby boy weighing 9lbs, who they named Jovan. Rowna was now in her twenties and got a job in a college teaching law. She worked full-time but had a helper that took care of the baby whilst she was at work, and did the cleaning. Jovan was quite fond of Shelly and she took good care of him. Unbeknown to Rowna, Shelley was helping out with other duties too which she would definitely not approve of.

It was a hot summer's day in June when Rowna fell ill at work and had to get a taxi home. She did not call her husband as she didn't want to disturb him at work. She would at least wait until he got home as she was not sick unto death. The black and yellow taxi picked her up from work and as the roads were not congested it took 30 minutes for her to arrive home. When she got to the front door she was about to ring the bell but thought maybe baby was sleeping as the house seemed quiet and so she opened the door with her key. As she slowly opened the door and closed it behind her and turned in the direction of the hallway, making her way through the living room she nearly fell over when she saw Jeff and Shelley making love on the white shag pile rug in the front room, naked as the day they were born. They froze when they saw Rowna, then Shelley grabbed her clothes and ran out of the front door, forgetting her shoes.

Rowna, once she got her breath back, stepped past Jeff and went to the baby's room to check on him. Jovan was sleeping in his cot and so Rowna slowly sat next to the chair by his cot and cried silently as she was not feeling well anyway and was in shock. Jeff knocked on the door and Rowna said in a quiet voice as the baby was still asleep, "Get lost and move the hell away from me, you slimy sorry ass of a man." Jeff realised that it was best to leave her alone for the time being and so he went for a long drive in his van.

Shelley never went back and Rowna did not attempt to find her, however, for Jeff the nightmare began. Rowna gave him the silent treatment for weeks. It was the talk of the neighbourhood for weeks as neighbours saw Shelly running up the road whilst trying to get her clothes on because she ran from the house naked since she did not have time to put them on. Shelly was the local slacker so this type of behaviour was very much expected of her but they felt sorry for Rowna because she was a respectable person and now Grandma Pearle had gone she kept her business to herself, and so wouldn't divulge her private life with the neighbours or anyone for that matter.

She had to find a new helper but this time she found a helper who was 60, respectable and was married too. Rowna felt that she could not trust the male species anymore and so lost interest in her husband. She tolerated him for Jovan's sake but things were never the same again. Intimacy became a ritual and so she had to put great effort in carrying out those wifely duties.

The rumour started spreading that Jeff was the man of the

town, being tall and handsome. The local easy-going girls were lining up to get a piece of the action and Jeff was not going to turn them down; he conquered Shelley because she was an easy catch in the beginning and she is what was known as a 'hot gal'. If the truth be told word is that Jeff set up Shelley to apply for the job in his home so that he could have his way with her when he fancied a bit of 'slap and tickle'. He boasted to his friends that he had the wife and the concubine under one roof.

Jeff was to encounter more affairs whilst being married to Rowna but she didn't care anyway because her plan was to move on with her life as soon as she was able to save enough money to finance her travels to Canada. Rowna continued further studies part-time, qualifying to become a barrister, and she graduated with her Master's Degree in Law. Once she had accomplished this she asked Jeff for a divorce. Jovan was eight years old at the time and so he was reluctant to agree to the divorce but after some negotiation in terms of property and money he felt the settlement was fair.

The marriage had broken down but with Rowna's integrity and principles instilled in her by Grandma Pearle, which she valued and was not willing to let go of, she allowed Jeff to remain in the property as it was mortgage free, plus she had planned to take Jovan with her. Rowna did not tell Jeff the whole story though, because she had met a friend, named Bill, who lived in Canada whilst working at the college and he had agreed to help her get settled in her new intended place of residence (Canada) on her arrival.

Bill was visiting a friend at the college when he bumped into Rowna and somehow managed to spill coffee down the front of her white transparent blouse. Luckily for Rowna the coffee wasn't hot, it was warm, and Bill offered her his gold silk handkerchief to wipe it from her clothes. Bill felt awkward but after catching his breath he helped Rowna to pick her books up from the ground where they were scattered as she dropped them whilst trying to protect her clothes from coffee stains. He then offered to give her a lift home so she could change her top and then take her back. They talked and in so doing she realised that Bill was friendly and as she didn't have many friends this seemed like an opportunity to start what seemed like a good friendship. Rowna was right because she was able to talk to him about many things that she was unable to share with Jeff and he would listen and give her great advice. He at times gave Rowna encouragement to keep going through her difficult period in her marriage. Jeff sleeping out at times did not help, plus he did not help to care for Jovan and treated her like she was his enemy rather than his wife. Rowna remembered Grandma Pearle's warning about Jeff and without any doubt her premonition was correct.

Eventually the marriage hit rock bottom and Rowna filed for a divorce as she didn't see the point in prolonging the headaches and heartaches she was facing on a daily basis. Jeff was happy with life the way they were and Rowna had had enough of the excuses and disappointments, especially as his behaviour was now beginning to affect Jovan with all the empty promises made and failing to support his son in school activities such as football practice and parents' evening meetings.

Chapter 5

Rowna Lands in Canada

It was the spring of 1992 when Rowna finally landed on Canadian soil. She held Jovan's hand as they walked through immigration looking for Bill who was to meet them at the airport and take them to a hotel close by where Bill lived in Toronto. She could not help but admire her surroundings because foreign sure looked different; there were people of different nationalities all around her and everyone seemed to be going about their business without noticing each other. Rowna smiled when she spotted Bill and he reached out and gently hugged her as she approached him. Jovan waved at Bill who waved back and gently patted him on the head.

The hotel was 20 miles away from the airport and she got there late evening. Rowna was fascinated by the view and her surroundings, she kept pinching herself to assure herself that she was actually in Canada and not just dreaming, she had waited long enough for this very day. She grinned and said, "I think I made a good decision and I am going to love it here."

She had just enough time to look for an apartment before

she started her new job which she applied for whilst in Jamaica and was successful in securing the position as a barrister in a law firm.

It took Rowna a week to find a two-bedroom apartment and also to find a good school for Jovan to attend. Jovan was a sociable boy and it didn't take him long to settle and make new friends. Bill took charge in assisting Rowna by showing her and Jovan around Canada, mainly at the weekends. He drove a white customised Lamborghini and had access to more than one prestigious car as and when required for various functions. He encouraged Rowna to take driving lessons, empowering herself in being able to get around independently with her son because he knew Rowna would be happier as she was an independent woman of integrity and she needed a car for work purposes too. Jovan at first found it difficult to understand the accent of his new friends and my guess is that his friends had to adjust to his too, but as always children have a language in common and that is playing with each other without any difficulties. Jovan was to become a popular student in his school by the time he graduated.

Rowna followed Bill's advice and booked lessons with a local driving school. Within six months of starting her driving lessons she took her test and passed first attempt. She bought a white Toyota 4 Series and had no regrets in so doing. Rowna found a friend, a brother and a confidant in Bill. He never complained when she required his help and as a matter of fact he often volunteered to assist and aid her when she needed it.

Jovan was growing fond of Bill even though he kept in touch with his biological father in Jamaica who was now married to slack Shelley and they had a two-year-old child together. Bill eventually asked Rowna to marry him, but this was not done in any ordinary way!

Chapter 6

Bill Proposes

Christmas 1997 was a special year and season for the couple as Bill proposed to Rowna, but he did this publicly which almost knocked Rowna off her feet. After their Christmas meal, Bill had a friend call his mobile to say that they needed to come over to his house immediately as he had an emergency situation. Bill, Jovan and Rowna hurried to the place where Bob, his friend, was waiting patiently with Bill's family and their friends to surprise Rowna. When they got to the address there was a banner which was lit with the message 'ROWNA MY LOVE, WILL YOU MARRY ME?' Rowna was so surprised that she froze at first and then burst into tears but this time not with sorrow, instead with unspeakable joy. She stepped out of the car where Bill had already alighted and opened the door for her. Going down on his left knee Bill proposed, presenting her with a huge diamond ring. She kissed him as he slipped the ring onto her left 'ring finger'. Jovan of course was in on the surprise and so he burst into laughter. Rowna's answer was definitely a yes and they then walked towards the door of the building where they were greeted by friends and family who congratulated them as they were watching from the window when Rowna agreed to marry Bill.

The engagement party went on till the early hours of the morning. The hall was packed with Bill's family and friends and some of Rowna's work colleagues. They partied into the early hours and Bill did not scrimp on impressing his fiancée as the table was spread with quality food and beverages, plus the hall was beautifully decorated and the caterers were sourced from the 'cream of the crop'.

Bill was a tall, dark and handsome man who was an entrepreneur and ran his own plant and machinery company. He came from a wealthy background of self-made millionaires and he was divorced so could relate to Rowna when she told him about the problems she was facing in her marriage as well as give her valuable support.

The wedding took place in Los Angeles and it was the talk of the town for weeks as many influential people attended the wedding, as you can imagine, as his family were business tycoons and Rowna had now formed friendships with some of these people. As well as being a barrister she had work colleagues and acquaintances.

Jovan excelled in school and attended one of the best colleges in Toronto. He later graduated top of his class and left for university in England to pursue his four-year Engineering degree.

Rowna gave birth to a gorgeous baby girl (Paris) in her late 30s, whom you can imagine lacked nothing in terms of wealth and wellbeing. She was lavished with gifts and loved by all her family, particularly by her dad and her big brother Jovan. Paris was Bill's only biological child but he also adopted Jovan.

Chapter 7

Rowna's Secret Revealed

In 2004 Rowna went back to Jamaica to build a tomb for her grandmother who was buried in Calvary Cemetery. This was something that Rowna believed was necessary as a token of her love for Grandma Pearle and to ensure that her grandma would never totally be forgotten. Bill attended to support Rowna as he knew how much she loved and respected her grandmother. On her arrival she repaired the house that she inherited from Grandma Pearle and by then it was empty because Jeff and Shelley had bought their own property when they got married and moved in together. She extended the property to five bedrooms and added extras (garage, veranda, extend kitchen, dining room) to make it look fantastic. She also had one of Grandma Pearle's wedding pictures supersized and hung in the refurbished living room.

When all was completed she let the property so as to keep it inhabited and maintained. The tomb she got designed and made for Grandma Pearle was made from marble and her picture was engraved on it in colour with Grandma's favourite bible scripture inscribed in 'French script'.

Rowna had one secret she did not tell anyone including her 'soulmate' Bill. She intended to take it to her grave but it was truly bothering her because as well as being raped there was the abortion which she had experienced because Uncle Neville impregnated her. This haunted her dreams and it was disturbing her peace mentally. She had managed to stay sane because she was strong willed and knew from receiving counselling that this was not her fault and she had no control over the situation; at the time this happened as she was a minor.

However, she had to put closure to this matter as there was an individual who was accountable and he was still living in make-believe and thought that he had gotten away with what he did. Finally Rowna decided to share her 'secret' with Bill who was very sympathetic and supportive. Rowna herself being a barrister now was able to see justice done. Rowna made an unannounced visit to see her uncle and confronted him about the issue which he tried to deny at first instance, trying to hide his shameful act, but when Rowna took him to court, he finally confessed not only to Rowna's case but to other young girls whom he had sexually abused and in some case destroyed their lives because they got pregnant and were thrown out of their parental homes. Two of them had carried his babies to full term and gave them up for adoption.

Uncle Neville's conscience finally caught up with him and he went to prison for his crimes, but after serving five years of his 15-year sentence he was found dead in his cell at the age of 65 and the reason for death was unexplained.

Uncle Neville's wife was so ashamed of her husband's behaviour, she apologised to all the victims, including myself, who were now grown, and compensated them financially which she felt was the least she could do to show remorse for her husband's cruelty. Some of the young ladies started an organisation to help support rape victims, offering counselling services and legal advice.

Rowna's story is one of many rape cases, but she had a destiny to fulfil and did not give up even though she had to face some unpleasant situations. She shared her story with many young girls who were abused at a young age and as a result their true characters were tarnished and most suffered in silence. The world is waking up to this now and that is progress. No one should have to go through such psychological and physical abuse, especially when they had no say in the matter and were totally innocent.

Rowna can now look back at her early beginnings when she had the inner feeling that she was born to be 'somebody of importance'. She held on to that thought. Likewise we are all born for a purpose and regardless of what it is, our ultimate fulfilment will come when we have fulfilled that which we were destined and purposed for.

Chapter 8

Rowna Reunites with Annette

Rowna regularly travelled for work purposes as some of her prestigious clients were based in various different countries. One particular client who had a huge account with the firm she worked for had a substantial claim in monetary terms made against his conglomerate company and so she had to travel urgently for a few days to New York. Whilst she was dining at the Hilton in New York, she heard a familiar voice calling her name from behind. When she looked around, lo and behold it was Loudmouth Lucy, who was now elegant and no longer a brawl. Lucy gave her a hug and joined her in having brunch, engaging in conversations about the old times. Lucy was the hotel manager and was doing well for herself. She was not married but was living together with her partner in a four-bedroom house in New York. She had no children of her own and did not plan to have any either.

Lucy shared some important information with Rowna which would help her piece together her genetics. Lucy's mother had died and so she went back to Jamaica to bury her.

At the funeral she was introduced to a well-dressed and elegant lady who wanted to speak with her. Two days after the funeral Lucy agreed to visit her in her home; when she got to the house she noticed that it was the house that Rowna had lived in with her grandmother, but it was refurbished and quite upmarket in appearance. She knocked on the door and the lady she met at the funeral opened it with greetings. They sat down over a cup of tea and buns and she made her enquiries to Lucy.

Lucy was surprised to know who the lady was. Her name was Annette and she was Rowna's mother. She asked if Annette knew where she was as she heard that both girls attended school together. Unfortunately, Lucy was not aware of Rowna's whereabouts as she left Jamaica before Rowna did. However, Lucy told Rowna's mum that she had heard that she was living somewhere in Canada and she had divorced from her husband Jeff some time ago. Lucy could only inform her of what she heard from others and unfortunately could shed no light on where in Canada Rowna was living, if indeed she was still living there.

Lucy told Rowna all she could which left Rowna with all types of emotions. Her mother had supposedly been staying in her property in Jamaica without her awareness for over two years and her mother had no idea that she was the landlord. Sure, her mother must have known that Grandma Pearle had died, but why return now?

Rowna thanked Lucy for the information she shared and exchanged contact details as she realised that Lucy was the only friend she had, really, whom she could trace back from childhood. Lucy shared some history with her, especially those back in Jamaica, and that was special to Rowna. They agreed to meet up in the near future and Rowna told her all about her life and that she had two children (a son with her first husband Jeff) and was now married to Bill and they too had a little girl.

Rowna had time to think and so by the time she got back home to her family in Canada, she had made up her mind to travel back to Jamaica to see her mother. She had some unanswered questions to put forward to her and regardless of what the outcome was, she was prepared as she had a family of her own now with strong bonds.

She spoke to Bill about it and he advised that she travelled to see her mother on her own but should she need him he would take the next available flight out to join her, plus Paris was still in school and so it was best for one of them to stay and take care of her. Rowna packed her suitcase and booked her flight after taking a week's leave from work. Whilst sitting in first class on British Airways to Norman Manley Airport in Kingston, Jamaica, Rowna thought of what she would say when she met Annette but regardless of the way she was going to say it, it had to be said.

Rowna got to the airport quite late so she booked in at the Sheraton Hotel and stayed the night. The next day she took a cab from the hotel, bought a fruit basket and headed for home. She had keys to the property but thought it would be more polite to ring the doorbell. A lady who fit the description of who Lucy described stood at the door. The lady froze and tears ran down her cheek. She beckoned to Rowna to come in with her hands and somehow Rowna knew this was her long-lost mother.

Annette sat down so as not to fall over. Rowna sat opposite her in the living room. Rowna said, "Hello, how are you?" to break the ice as Annette continued to sob.

Annette replied, "I am sorry, please forgive me."

Rowna paused and said, "Dry your tears and let me get you a glass of water." She gave her the fruit basket and said, "This is for you." Rowna got the water and handed the glass to Annette who slowly drank it down. They both hugged and after sobbing emotionally together they finally sat and talked.

Annette explained that whilst in New York she got

involved in drugs within the first six months because of her partner who invited her to the United States and sent her the ticket to travel. She did not realise that he was a drug dealer as he told her otherwise. As they were poor, she felt it was a good opportunity to make something of her life and send for Rowna as well as her parents. The long and short of it is that Annette was ashamed of her life and she could not tell her parents what she was doing for fear of breaking their hearts. After six months of living dangerously in the drugs arena, during a police raid she was locked up in prison for selling and dealing drugs and given a 20-year prison sentence.

Once she served the time she was released but deported back to Jamaica. Upon return to Jamaica she did not know how to face her family; being that she was a disgrace and being that her mother was such a proud woman she did not want to cause further humiliation to her. She lived in Manchester for eight years and then could bear it no longer so she decided to visit and when she arrived she realised that her parents had both died and her daughter had migrated. She rented the place and made enquiries as to who owned the property now but they did not disclose the owner as they said the owner wanted to remain anonymous. She explained that she had met Lucy but she did not know exactly where Rowna was either. Annette had also tried to find Jeff but he left no forwarding address with the neighbours when he moved out, so the only hope was that one day Rowna would return for vacation.

Rowna then explained to her mother that Lucy was the one she got the information about her from, and so Lucy did manage to reunite them in some strange way. She laughed and said to her mother, "Well it looks like Lucy's big mouth was a blessing and not a curse." They laughed at the joke.

Rowna over the next few days told her mother her life story and she took her to see both graves of her parents. Annette cried and laid flowers on them. Rowna took the house back from the estate agents and gave her mother permission to stay and live there rent free because as far as Rowna was concerned Annette had as much right to live there as she did.

Annette visited Rowna and her family from time to time but as Annette was growing old she did not want to live in a cold country, so she visited yearly in the summer. She got to know Jovan and Paris who adored her. Bill accepted Annette as his mother-in-law because he felt that she had suffered enough and after all, we are all human beings who are prone to make mistakes in our lives. The challenge is how we overcome them and move on with our lives whilst striving to be better people and learning from our errors and experience.

Rowna did not know her father and no one ever discussed him in anyway. However, Rowna did manage in conversation to ask her mother who her father was. Reluctantly she divulged who he was. She told Rowna that he was a married man who raped her at the age of 17 and he was locked up for his dirty deeds. He served time in prison and paid for his crime because she was brave enough to report him to the police. Tests were carried out and it was proven so the courts sentenced him to a long-term prison sentence. She decided to have the child because of her parents' Christian values and anti-abortion policy but she wanted the father to have no contact whatsoever.

Rowna told her mother her own story about her Uncle Neville and her mother commended her for seeking justice and succeeding in her case against him. She also knew she was not the only one to go through such an ordeal as her own mother did too and in both cases justice was done. Rowna never enquired about her father again as she lost total interest; as a matter of fact she was glad she did not get the chance to meet him because there are a few words she would have liked to say which were not pleasant at all.

Chapter 9

Bill's Misadventure

Business Tycoon Bill journeyed to various parts of the world. He travelled to Orlando, Florida, on business to meet with a potential client at the Waldorf Astoria Hotel where he booked an executive suite for two nights.

The hotel phone rang whilst Bill was having his shower; he wrapped the fluffy white towel around his waist with water trickling down his muscular spine and sweetly scented body, and moved towards the brown Milena Chesterfield sofa where the phone was located to answered it. "Good morning Mr Diago; Mr Lorenzo is downstairs waiting in the lounge area for you," said the receptionist at the front desk.

Bill replied in his husky voice, "Please let him know I will be there in 15 minutes." He then put the phone down and hurried to get dressed.

Bill made his way towards the lift which was already waiting on his floor and he got off at the ground floor where he could see Jack waiting, holding what looked like a cup of coffee in his hand. "Sorry to have kept you waiting, Jack," said Bill as he shook his hand.

Jack was from Texas as could be depicted by his voice as he had a strong accent; he replied, "No trouble at all, Bill, it's my pleasure." They then had breakfast as it was still mid-morning.

They sat at a comfortable seat in the restaurant and ordered the chef's breakfast special on the menu. Jack's hat, which looked more like a cowboy's hat, took up half the table. They spoke shrewd business at the table as Jack was known for his wheeler-dealer technique in negotiating contracts and Bill was already aware of this so was prepared to compromise to win the business. They both struck a deal by the end of breakfast which lasted two hours. They shook hands on the deal and contract was agreed and signed in principle provided the necessary adjustment which Bill agreed to was carried out, then signed, sealed and delivered.

Jack left the hotel at 11:50am and Bill headed back to his room where he made the adjustments to the terms of the agreement and emailed it over to his personal assistant using his laptop, to check, correct any typo errors and send over to his lawyer to look it over.

It was at 2:45pm that Bill left the hotel room to go for his daily walk; he remembered the time because he looked down at his Rolex Daytona watch worn on his left wrist to check the time as he was schedule for a massage at 4pm. He wanted to make sure he would be back in time to keep the appointment.

Bill left the hotel lobby within five minutes of checking his watch and briskly walked to a nearby park. He stopped to get some water from a store as it was a hot day and sweat was seeping from his face. He walked for half an hour and then jogged back to the hotel. When he got back at 3:45pm he was greeted by two detectives, smartly dressed; they requested to speak to him as a matter of urgency which did not leave Bill much time to cancel his 4pm appointment.

Bill was bemused as he had no idea what they needed to speak to him about but being professional he invited them back to his room so as to maintain privacy. He offered the detectives cold drinks which they politely refused. Bill offered them a seat and he sat down trying to stay calm but feeling a bit anxious. The detective, who was about 6ft 2ins tall with short, black, shiny, gelled hair and smoothly shaven, stood up and proceeded to ask the question, "Where were you at 1:00pm today?" Bill thought the question was strange but he had nothing to hide so he explained he was in his hotel room working on a contract to send to his personal assistant. The detective asked various other questions which all seemed to be personally monitoring his movements that day. Bill then asked the detectives why they were questioning him and where this was leading to. There was a moment of silence where the detectives looked at each other. The other detective, who had not said a word up until that moment, told Bill that the man he had breakfast with, Jack Lorenzo, was found dead about three hours ago close to the hotel, and they found on his cadaver a card with Bill's details and a bill with the hotel address on it. This made Bill the number one suspect in this case as it appeared that Jack was shot and killed in a drive-by shooting within minutes of leaving the hotel.

Bill explained that he was due to leave the hotel room the next morning as he had a flight booked to get back home. The detective asked him not to leave Orlando until they checked out his story and gave him the all-clear. When the detective left Bill's room he decided to call Rowna and ask for her advice since he was a possible murder suspect and she was his barrister. Jack was a known wheeler-dealer in business but apart from that nothing else showed up on his rigorous background check which Bill carried out before agreeing to engage in business with him, which was a standard procedure for the company.

Rowna booked the next available flight to Orlando to join her husband as she knew that in cases such as these Bill would need to have a barrister to represent him should he be charged. Rowna also advised Bill to give no further evidence until she got there, which was the next day. Bill found himself in a murder investigation rather than closing a business deal and this was somewhat bizarre as he had not left the hotel room but for an hour to take his daily exercise.

Bill was not feeling particularly hungry that evening so he had a ham and cheese baguette before retiring for the night.

Early the following morning Bill went to the front desk where he checked into the hotel and asked if their closed-circuit surveillance camera recording for the past two days was available for his perusal and they told him that the recording was taken by the detectives. Bill felt confident that surely they would be able to check the time he left and returned to the hotel. Bill thanked the receptionist for the information and sat in the lounge to read the local paper; without fail Jack Lorenzo's murder was in the headlines, and thankfully he was not mentioned but there was mention of a possible suspect.

Rowna got to the hotel at 5:30pm that evening which brought relief to Bill as he was alone and needed support. Rowna immediately made a few calls and before long the two detectives who visited the day before were back at the hotel, this time with Rowna present and asking questions of her own. The detectives knew that Rowna was one that knew the law and was not to be challenged as she had influential contacts. The detectives assured Rowna that the recordings from the hotel were being verified and that Bill would be informed of the outcome by the end of the day.

At 9:00pm whilst the couple were having their evening meal as they waited anxiously in Bill's suite, the awaited phone call came which verified and confirmed the answers Bill gave the detectives of his whereabouts on the day Jack was murdered. Bill's movements were no longer under scrutiny as he had only left the hotel for approximately one hour and Jack was already dead before he went for his walk.

Further background checks eliminated Bill as a possible suspect as he had no known motive to kill Jack. That was a close call for Bill and so Rowna advised him to take an assistant with him in the future when he travelled outside Canada to do business. Bill knew his wife was more than competent to take the case; without any further delay they got the next flight out of Orlando Sanford International Airport heading home to Canada.

Following up on the case a few weeks later, it was revealed that Jack Lorenzo's murderers were caught and the story was unfolded that it was one of Jack's business associates (Matt) who paid a professional hitman to assassinate him. Jack was in the process of negotiating a takeover bid which if he was successful was going to be a threat to Matt's insider dealings being exposed as the auditors had raised some concerns in their earlier consultations. Matt felt getting rid of Jack would have stopped the takeover procedures but in fact it only delayed the process. Matt failed to meet the assassinator's demands, who raised the fee when he realised that the stakes were high if he in turn blackmailed Matt for hush money. Matt refused to adhere to the demand and as a result word was leaked and the perpetrators were caught and given long prison sentences. Matt knew that Jack was travelling to Orlando to meet Bill so he hired the hitman who followed Jack when he left the hotel and murdered him.

Chapter 10

Rowna's Unannounced Visitor

Rowna had a very busy work schedule due to the high-profile clientele she managed in her job. She was constantly travelling and hardly had time to correspond with old friends. Bill had a great idea and so got in touch with her oldest friend who was still residing in New York; yes, you guessed right, Loudmouth Lucy! Bill explained to Lucy that he felt Rowna needed some time away as she seemed a little stressed of late, and was not her usual jovial self. He planned to make arrangements with her work partner to book her a week off and asked Lucy to help set up a surprise holiday break for Rowna where they could catch up on old times. Lucy was owed some holiday from her job and so felt it was a great idea and as money was not an issue then the world was her oyster. It was just a matter of making some enquiries with a selection of travel agents and making a choice.

Once Lucy put the phone down she immediately started to make arrangements and felt honoured that Rowna's millionaire tycoon would choose to trust her to escort his wife on a 'girlfriend only' holiday and not forgetting, this was a complimentary all-paid holiday and to put the icing on the cake it would be one that only the elite could afford. In monetary terms she would have to save up for a lifetime to be able to afford such a holiday. Well, after searching the net high and low, Lucy's choice was Necker Island, a British Virgin Island owned by Sir Richard Branson located in the Caribbean. She wasted no time in making reservations for two flying from Canada as she wanted to surprise Rowna, turning up unannounced couple of days before they ventured out together. Lucy confirmed with Bill and he was happy with her choice, in fact he didn't feel that him making the choice would have topped Lucy's own. The flight and board was paid via a World Elite Mastercard owned only by the privileged few.

Bill had managed to swing things his way, getting Rowna the time off for the trip and Lucy's visit. Rowna's business partner was in on the surprise so had to find a way to allow her the time off without her suspecting anything and that was not going to be easy as she had to know everything happening around her.

Her business partner told Rowna that there was a new client account that they were trying to source, and the client insisted that Rowna was the partner she wanted to see and that she wanted the first meeting to be held at Rowna's home on Saturday, which was a couple of days away. Rowna reluctantly agreed but after making some enquiries of her own about the client's collateral and worth she could not pass up an opportunity like that. The truth is that the client was due to land the firm a huge account doing business with them but her partner had already arranged to meet with the client. However, that is the only way that Rowna would agree to stay at home.

Lucy was all packed and travelled overnight on the Friday and so Bill left early the Saturday morning to pick her up without disclosing the surprise to Rowna as she thought he was going to pick up the client. Lucy wore a bright red pant suit and so she wasn't hard for Bill to spot in the airport. Bill beckoned to her to come over to where he was waiting and welcomed this woman he had never met, that his wife spoke so much about ever since they met in New York.

Lucy, as always, was happy and smiling though Bill could not understand why Rowna nicknamed her Loudmouth Lucy because she sure was very polite and graceful. They soon started their journey back to the house but whilst Lucy sat in the passenger side in the front of the car she couldn't help but think how lucky her friend was to catch such a big fish who drove a Lamborghini with white leather interior and who was tall and handsome.

Bill pulled up outside the gate and hit the remote control button attached to the car; the gate opened and he drove into a car park with a variety of other cars parked there too. Lucy thought to herself, *I am sure his extended family lives here too.* Bill opened the car door for Lucy and gave her his hand to help her out of the car; she smiled as she held his hand and dismounted the car. Lucy mumbled under her breath, "It's a pity you're married to my friend because I would sure find a way to make you mine."

Bill asked, "Did you say something, Lucy?"

Lucy smiled and said, "No, not a word."

Rowna was busy getting ready for her client and preparing breakfast. Bill opened the door and Lucy walked in. Rowna almost fell backwards in amazement as she could not believe her eyes. She ran and hugged Lucy and welcomed her into her humble abode. "More like palace!" shouted Lucy as she giggled. She looked at Bill, who was standing on the other side of the lounge by then and had a huge grin on his face, and said to him that he was in on this surprise and she thanked him.

The ladies spoke all evening and then Lucy told her that she was going to be staying for a while and would be escorting her on her surprise vacation which was to take place on Monday morning. Well, knowing Rowna, she never stopped pestering Lucy until she revealed where they would both be going. Rowna was overwhelmed with her choice and could not wait to get away; she soon forgot about work and was now in the mood to go off with Lucy and enjoy her week away.

Lucy spent Sunday helping her friend to get ready for the vacation; they had an emergency hair appointment for them both and shopped for clothes and essentials for the suitcases. Monday morning could not come soon enough for them and Bill drove them to the airport to catch the private jet to Necker Island.

The ladies had a great time away and enjoyed the sand, sea, weather and the fresh healthy food. Lucy had never had such luxury, though Rowna was quite acquainted with this standard of living as money was never an issue, it was more 'where should we go this time?' Lucy and Rowna talked about school days and their childhood and they even spoke about Grandma Pearle and her old-fashioned ways, however, Rowna added that it was her grandma's effort and consistency that moulded her into the woman she became and that the only regret she had was that Grandma Pearle was no longer living so she could garnish her with luxury and the high standard of living that she herself now enjoyed.

When the vacation was over both ladies returned to their homes but it was a time spent together on a luxurious island that they would never forget. Those two friends shared memories which proved to them that 'it is not how you start that matters but where you finish'. The two friends kept in touch though they both had busy lives because some friends are irreplaceable especially when your history goes back a long way.

Chapter 11

Rowna's Stalker

The mobile phone rang and Rowna quickly moved towards it. Her mobile was sitting on top of the mantelpiece in the upstairs hallway. She got to the phone just as the answering service kicked in. "Hello?" she answered and no one spoke but she could hear heavy breathing followed by a click. The caller had hung up. Rowna did not react as she felt it was probably a prank call or just someone playing a joke; she pressed call back which accessed a recording that said, "You have dialled an incorrect number," so Rowna thought no more of it.

Rowna went to work as usual and once she got home the mobile phone rang again with a private number display, same as earlier that day. Rowna, being used to clients calling all hours of the day still had no reason for concern but when she answered the call, once again the caller was breathing heavily on the other end of the phone. Rowna took the phone to her husband who was laying down in their bedroom, gave the phone to him and asked him to listen. The caller, hearing a man's voice instead of Rowna's hung up immediately.

Bill, being concerned as this had never happened before, asked Rowna if she'd had any confrontation with anyone or was aware of any strange occurrences recently. Rowna could not think of anyone that she had offended personally; yes, her job as a barrister was one who upheld the law but not directly her fights. Bill out of concern asked Rowna to report it to the police as this was intolerable and also he did not want her to be at risk especially when she had no idea who was making the calls and why.

Rowna waited until the next morning which was her morning off from work. The sun was shining brightly and the birds sang melodiously in the nearby trees; so much appreciated after the long, cold winter months that had just gone by. Spring had sprung and Rowna was feeling perky so she decided to walk to the nearby police station after dropping Paris off at school. Rowna noticed a short, muscular man following behind her from a distance and he was wearing dark glasses and a baseball cap with a grey Mac coat, which was what made her felt suspicious of the man in the first place.

She recalled him standing across the road from her home as she left with Paris but took no notice of him as he wasn't directly paying attention to her. She knew the neighbours were away on vacation, but thought it may have been a passer-by. However, she spotted him once again after dropping Paris on the opposite side of the road and she thought, *That seems a bit odd.*

He must have realised that she was approaching the police station so he diverted because Rowna once outside their office turned to look for him and he was nowhere to be found. Rowna felt it best to mention her suspicions to the sergeant whom she reported the incident to as a formal complaint.

The officers told Rowna to avoid travelling alone if possible, but to also equip herself with pepper spray and take precautions such as asking a colleague to assist her to her car when leaving work and when she got to her destinations she should either have someone meet her by her car or if possible to have an escort to accompany her until they were able to investigate the matter.

Bill, being of high influence in his business circle wasted no time in getting a private detective on the case to ensure his wife was safe. However, the man Rowna actually saw following her was not exactly the mystery caller; in fact he was the private investigator that Bill hired to protect her.

The short muscular man in the green Mac was in fact Private Investigator (PI) Sharky who had an excellent track record of solving the mysterious cases he took on. The calls kept coming but the duration of the calls were not long enough to locate the culprit, plus the numbers frequently changed as the police discovered. Rowna was determined to get on with her life as normally as she possibly could, given the circumstances, but somehow the atmosphere was tense.

Three weeks had gone by and finally Rowna received a C4-sized envelope with no return address. She opened the letter and it was different from any other letter she had seen. The printed letters were cut from a magazine to form a sentence which read, "I know your every move and you cannot escape from me; I always conquer and never fail." The letter was passed on to the police but not before the private investigator was able to scrutinise its contents.

PI Sharky just had to be sure that the envelope that Rowna received was the one that he witnessed the suspect, who he had been observing for a few days now, drop inside the letter box near the office where Rowna worked. PI Sharky noticed that Rowna never received the calls during office hours and somehow the stalker knew the times his victim would be at home so would call around those times or before she attended work. If the stalker intended to attack his victim the time of day he called should have been random but this was not the case. The stalker probably worked in an office as the victim did and so did not want to draw attention when he made the calls. PI Sharky suspected that Rowna had a relationship with the caller but the type of relationship had to be determined.

PI Sharky, after viewing the letter and taking photos of it, immediately visited Rowna's place of work and asked that the cleaners delay emptying the bins. When he checked all the bins in the offices he saw a magazine that had letters cut out from it and this was to help solve the mystery of the case. The bin was underneath the desk of a colleague that Rowna worked with. The magazine was taken as evidence and the colleague was not informed so as to ensure he would be arrested upon the evidence gathered identifying him as the stalker.

Ryan Corpel was a lawyer who had recently joined the company. He was in training under Rowna's supervision. He had a crush on Rowna, who was unaware of the situation and did not give that idea a thought as he showed her no obvious signs. Ryan craftily had his plan but unfortunately being from another state the firm was not aware of this behaviour in a previous incident with a student some years earlier whilst he was studying for his law degree. However, the case was dropped as it could not be proven. PI Sharky did some investigation about Ryan once he became a suspect on his list.

The private investigator took the magazine cuttings he took from the bin to the police station where the letter was held and they were satisfied that the letters were taken from the exhibit as the cuttings fit perfectly. Now that the suspect had been identified it was time to apprehend him. The police wasted no time as they were not sure what exactly this man was capable of, being that he was not charged for the offence the first time, which it seems highly likely that he could have committed. He may now have felt that he was above the law and would once again get away with it, and prepared to go further by even abducting his victim this time around.

PC Rogers and PI Sharky visited the suspect's home and arrested him after obtaining a warrant. Luckily for Rowna he pleaded guilty as he saw that the evidence was strong against him being that they collected several phones and SIM cards bearing Rowna's mobile number which were in his possession at the time of his arrest.

PI Sharky was not given that name for fun; but for the very nature that it portrays. He got his 'man' and could now close the case leaving the police and the court to carry out justice.

Rowna could once again get on with her normal routine and in time she would forget the traumatic time she had facing her stalker daily without knowing.

Chapter 12

Paris Contracts Meningitis

The school rang Rowna's mobile and it was switched off so they rang Bill and were able to get hold of him. "Come straight away, Mr Diago, your daughter is running a high temperature and has to be collected as soon as possible." Bill jumped into his car and got to the school within a short space of time.

"Where is she?" Bill shouted to the school receptionist.

"The ambulance just left for The Cleveland Clinic, as was instructed via the phone by Mrs Diago who we managed to contact after speaking with you, because Paris's health was rapidly—"

Mr Diago got back into his car and started his journey to the hospital before the receptionist managed to finish her sentence.

As he walked inside the door of the clinic he saw his wife at the front desk registering their daughter as a matter of formality. A doctor came to meet them and told them that they were now trying to get the fever down as her temperature was rocketing by the minute. They also told them that they were running tests to determine Paris's condition and as soon as they got the results they would be able to apply the correct treatment.

The doctor assured them that their little girl was in safe hands and receiving the best possible care. Rowna was sobbing uncontrollably and so Bill had to try and calm her; by so doing he had to remain calm himself and so he had no time to think of the worst, he knew the family was depending on his strength to hold it together.

Some hours had passed and Bill suddenly forgot he hadn't called Jovan to let him know his sister was in hospital, so he called and though he did not get a reply he left a message on his mobile phone asking him to return his call. Bill called his parents and Rowna's mother to let them know the situation. Jovan did not return the call; instead he turned up at the hospital to support his family and to make enquiries about what was happening. At that time a surgeon walked towards the family and asked to speak to Mr and Mrs Diago in private.

"That was a close call. We have managed to stabilise the fever and we had to perform emergency surgery," said the surgeon.

"What's wrong with my daughter and how is she doing?" asked Bill in a fretful tone.

Doctor Dingo explained that Paris had contracted meningitis which caused both her temperature to rocket and rashes over her body. He stressed that due to acting quickly in getting her to the hospital they were able to save her life, but had they prolonged taking her to the hospital she might not have been so lucky. Rowna was so distressed but relieved knowing that her daughter was still alive. Paris was put in an isolation unit for a few days whilst recovering and to ensure that the illness was quarantined.

At first the family could only view her through a glass window but eventually they were able to have physical contact with her wearing protective gear. Paris was healing well and being a child she was resilient, so soon was back to her usual perky self.

It later came to light that two other children in Paris's school had the illness, one the day before and the other the day after Paris got ill. An immunisation programme was put in place to make sure all children attending the school who were not yet immunised against meningitis received vaccination against the disease.

Paris told her mother that she had a near-death experience whilst on the operating table. She told Rowna that she could see someone who looked just like her lying on the table below her and the doctors were busy attending to her lookalike whilst she was floating around the room singing Mary Had A Little Lamb, however, she noticed that no one could hear or see her. Then she saw an opening in the ceiling which she slipped into and once through the opening she could see someone with wings in a long white gown where a bright light began to shine. She floated towards the light but whilst going towards it she could hear someone calling her name. "Paris, stay with us!" shouted the doctor who had two big pieces of equipment in his hand that he put on the chest of her lookalike and she jumped and open her eyes.

"I then found myself diving back towards the bed and I was no longer floating above the doctors and above the ceiling but instead was back on the bed looking at some happy faces around me, but my lookalike had disappeared. I felt scared but sleepy and then I closed my eyes and I guess I must have fallen asleep because when I woke up I was no longer in that room but in a room with needles in my arms and machines around my bed making weird noises."

Rowna knew from the description Paris gave her that it could not have been just a dream. She told Bill, who was confused, and advised that they saw their own doctor and relayed what Paris had said. The doctor, though he had no expertise in such field could only advise that from past experience with other patients this was not unheard of, but to make sure to notify him of anything they may be worried about with her emotional or physical wellbeing. However, he had no immediate cause for concerns.

Paris returned to school after five weeks and continued to perform well academically. Unfortunately one child who contracted the disease died as he did not receive medical attention in time. The school made an outdoor bench in the play area with a plaque in memory of him – 'RIP Peter Swaby age 9'.

Chapter 13

Uncle Rupert Comes to Town

Bill's Uncle Rupert lived in Oklahoma with his wife Rebecca. They visited every five years for the family reunion party held in Vancouver where Bill's father, who is Rupert's brother, lives. Rupert owned several lumber yards where he built his empire and made his multimillions. Rupert's three children who also live in Vancouver with their family all came for the party. The family was quite big and lived in various parts of the planet and therefore this was a time when everyone would get to meet the new additions to the family, as well as honouring the older generations who were the founders of most of the business empire they owned.

Uncle Rupert was the eldest of the brothers still living and so he organised the reunion party with the help of his brothers and his wife and children. Uncle Rupert wanted this arrangement to be special because he was celebrating his 85th birthday, as well as he had a terminal illness and was not expecting to survive for the next family reunion, so he was going to make this one the best ever. Only Uncle Rupert's wife and siblings knew of his illness as he did not want it publicly known, neither did he welcome sympathy. He did not want to live the rest of his days out with people feeling sorry for him. He did not want their pity either; he just wanted everyone to see him as he was which was a fun-loving and adventurous being. The Fairmont Pacific Rim Hotel was the chosen place for the event after much debate. All the family were booked into rooms of their choice in the same hotel as the party was expected to continue into the early hours of the morning and therefore those with children could at least stay overnight.

Jovan finished his university degree that year and was on his way back from England for the big night out. The day was cloudy but that did not bother him as he was on his way to the sunnier part of the planet where he called home. "Toronto here I come!" Jovan yelled with outstretched hands. At that moment he heard a bang and shouting in terminal five of Heathrow Airport. The loud explosion caused confusion in everyone and people were running and screaming all over the airport first-class lounge. At that moment an announcement was made for everyone to stay calm and security were scurrying up and down the airport as though they were searching for something or someone.

Jovan grabbed hold of one of the security staff as he went by and asked, "What is going on?" He was told to keep low and hide if possible in the lounge area behind the bar until he was given further instructions. At this time Jovan was terrified because it appeared that some people a few feet away were lying helplessly with injuries and some were in pain as you could hear their cries for help. Jovan noticed a young boy sitting alone and clutching his left arm who was shouting for his mum, so he stayed low but moved towards the boy who obviously needed some support at the time. Jovan managed to calm him, but asked him to lie still. Jovan noticed not far from the boy a lady was lying very still, not moving, so he wondered whether it was the boy's mother. He made sure the child was comfortable and then moved towards the lady who was quite still. He used a mirror he carried in his pocket to put to her nose to determine whether she was still breathing, as he was not sure whether to move her as she was laying on her side.

He had to make an informed decision, so once he saw that she was still breathing he performed CPR procedures and laid her in the recovery position whilst shouting for help. At that moment security was close by so then came to assist the injured lady. He went back to stay with the child until the ambulance arrived and he was able to leave the boy in safe hands. They had to evacuate the airport and Jovan booked into the Hilton Hotel close by. Whilst listening to the news the reporter reported that a bomb was detonated in the airport and they suspect that it was a terrorist group who was responsible, but were unable to confirm at that time. Jovan was so shaken up that he rang his dad and told him what happened at the airport, so Bill hired a private jet to fly him back home the next morning as he was suffering from shock.

The following afternoon after the incident at Heathrow Airport, Jovan got back home safely where he saw his own GP who was able to prescribe the necessary medication.

Now the commotion was over, Jovan was still looking forward to meeting all his family members as he had not yet had the opportunity to meet the new additions. They included children and those who recently were married into the family, plus he had history lessons with the older generation who could enlighten him about past events that happened before he was born.

The big day finally arrived; the cars that lined the car park were classy ones and vintage ones too. Jovan's favourites were the 1958 Chevrolet Impala and the Rolls Royce Phantom III Wrath vintage. These cars were driven by Uncle Rupert's generation. The hall where the function took place was huge and beautifully decorated. The cakes were like nothing of this world and had seven tiers. Some of the champagnes being served were Dom Perignon, Bollinger, Perrier Jouet, Armand de Brignac and others. The decorations were very colourful with red, blue and yellow being the dominant colours. The music was of a mixture; contemporary country, renaissance, honky-tonk, traditional country, techno, reggae, Dixieland, folk rock and disco.

The party went on into the night and finally at about 12:30am Uncle Rupert gave his usual speech to congratulate everyone for making the effort to attend and to compliment them for looking so elegant and superbly dressed. He then made a toast to all his brothers and their families and his own wife and family. His speech was somewhat different this time around as he told everyone that as he was getting on in age he hoped that Bill's dad (Mike) who he expected to supersede him, being he was the youngest brother, would take over the family tradition for future events. Mike gave a toast in agreement and said, "I will try, but you are the original Big Bro." All the family clapped and laughed at the joke.

Though the event was for family some close friends were invited too, those that were seen as adopted family. Cynthia, who was a close friend of Bill because they grew up together in the same street and attended the same secondary school, had a daughter (Georgia) who had just turned 20 years old; she was present at the reunion and dressed elegantly in a pink satin pencil dress that clung to her body, displaying her full autonomy very tastefully. Jovan was drawn to her beauty and so could not keep his eyes off her all through the evening. Eventually he plucked up the courage to strike up a conversation when her handkerchief fell from her hand; he picked it up from the two-toned marble floor, where it fell, and handed it to her gently. He smiled and said, "You seems to have dropped this on purpose, but I don't mind picking it up for you."

She smiled and took it from his hand forcefully, then said, "You are Bill's son, aren't you?"

She chuckled and Jovan replied, "Yes, I believe I am." This led to a conversation that lasted throughout the evening into the early hours of the morning. By the end of the event they had exchanged numbers and decided to keep in touch for the future.

Bill and Rowna looked on as they watched Jovan and Georgia dance the night away. Rowna turned to Bill and said, "That young lady sure would be a great choice for our boy."

Bill turned to Rowna and said, "Let's not count our chickens before they hatch," and smirked at her.

Chapter 14

Uncle Rupert's Funeral

Uncle Rupert died three months later and his wife wrote in his eulogy that he had been terminally ill for nine months and died of prostate cancer. Aunt Rebecca also said in her speech that her husband did not want the younger members of the family to know because he did not want to be treated any differently; he wanted them to remember him as the fun-loving person he always was.

The black horse-drawn carriage pulled up outside St Monica Catholic Church in Edmond, Oklahoma, where Uncle Rupert lived. The 24-karat gold, obsidian black, luxury gilded casket glittered as the sun shone on it through the glass covering. The procession followed behind with the brothers and their families, tycoon friends, staff members, business associates and many more.

The four surviving brothers lifted the casket on their shoulders and carried Uncle Rupert's body into the church very slowly and in step with each other. The choir sang Bridge Over Troubled Water which was chosen by Mike and his brothers as the opening song. The atmosphere was sad and bleak and it felt as though time stood still for a moment.

Uncle Rupert was a well-known and loved man in the community as he was not just a business tycoon but a philanthropist with reputable credentials. Mike supported Aunt Rebecca and his nephews over that period as was expected of him being the oldest surviving brother.

The funeral service was hosted by the family diocese bishop and the order of service was dictated by Uncle Rupert in his last will and testament, so could not be contested by any of his successors. The church was full with some standing and the service lasted for one hour. Five hundred attended the church but that figure doubled at the hall in the afternoon where there was a gathering to celebrate his life. He was buried in a private family plot where his mother and father were laid to rest before him.

At 3pm the internment of Uncle Rupert's body was performed where the family said their goodbyes and sang his favourite hymn at his request, Abide With Me. Rowna was the lead singer in rendering this piece of music as she was a natural soprano and had an angelic voice. Tears ran down Bill's face as his wife sounded out the melody with such beautiful harmony. Jovan and Paris were given the opportunity to lay violets in the tomb where he was buried. The occasion was sad but the event went as planned which is all anyone could have hoped for.

The hall was decorated in mauve and white. The tables were beautifully laid and pictures of Uncle Rupert were hanged on the walls of the hall displaying different milestones in his life. There were pictures of him as a baby, a toddler, in his school uniforms, a graduation picture from university, pictures of him when he got married and some with members of his family and his staff. They were displayed in such a sequence that you could form a picture in your mind of his life story.

The food and drinks were plenty and the finest champagne, caviar, roast, vegetables and all the trimmings was served.

There was a barbeque for those who wanted to eat outdoors and those who wanted to give a speech in memory of Uncle Rupert were given five-minute slots to do so.

The evening went well and the family all mourned together for their loss. Mike by the end of the evening was intoxicated, as were the other brothers, with alcohol, so they all stayed over in local hotels which were booked in advance.

Georgia consoled Jovan throughout the duration of the funeral and the family accepted her as their own daughter so she felt quite welcome throughout the event.

Bill was concerned about Aunt Rebecca because Uncle Rupert and his aunt did most things together. He often told Bill that she was his soulmate and his best friend and that he didn't think he could have made his fortune in life without his faithful wife's input. Just as his brother depended on Aunt Rebecca, so it was vice versa. He had discussed with Rowna that he intended to invite her up shortly after the funeral had taken place for a few weeks so she would not feel alone, as her adult sons were busy working in the days.

Once the will was read a week later, Aunt Rebecca was able to join Bill and Rowna in Toronto and stayed for two weeks after which she returned home to Oklahoma to continue running the ranch and business until the boys were able to take on the responsibility full-time. Aunt Rebecca survived her husband for another 10 years and finally died of natural causes at the age of 92. She was laid to rest beside her husband and had outlived three of the remaining four brothers.

Mike survived his three brothers; two of them died in a helicopter tragedy together and the one died of cancer; however, he was not of excellent health but with daily medication he was well enough to run his company and continue his daily routines. Mike was the last of the brothers and died two years later from pneumonia, and was laid to rest beside his brothers in their family burial plot.

Chapter 15

Jovan and Georgia Tie the Knot

Georgia, now a qualified medical doctor practicing medicine in her own private surgery, finally accepted Jovan's fourth marriage proposal to her. She did not want to get married until she was sure and as she had achieved all the goals that she had targeted, she was now ready to settle down with the man she truly loved.

Jovan proposed to Georgia at dinner privately as he had been turned down three times already, so though he had not given up hope, he could not be sure that she would say yes this time round. The ring was a blue sapphire stone, Georgia's favourite jewel. She loved the ring and boasted to friends and family about her engagement to Jovan. The engagement party was done on a small scale as the wedding plan was six months away.

Jovan wanted a small family wedding in Jamaica and Georgia was happy with that but insisted that she had the fairytale wedding dress she always dreamt of and a Cinderella horse-drawn carriage to transport her on the day of her wedding. Jovan had no reservations to Georgia's request as he knew it was her big day and she deserved the wedding of her dreams. Only close friends and family were invited, and Grandma Annette, who was still residing in Jamaica but was unable to travel as she had grown frail and was not able to manage long-distance travelling. Jovan did not correspond with his father, Jeff, because he failed in his eyes to play the role of a caring father in his life, so he did not inform his father or invite him to the wedding.

Rowna tried to encourage Jovan to change his mind and invite Jeff but he remained adamant that the only father that mattered to him was Bill. Bill was to be his best man.

It was the summer of 2014 that the wedding was arranged for. The hall was booked in Mandeville and the wedding was to be performed in a local church, the caterers were booked, the five-tier cake was ordered and made of the finest ingredients; Jamaica rum cake. Most of the plans were overseen by Grandma Annette who was proud of her grandson and his wife-to-be.

Grandma Annette attended a Pentecostal church and so she asked her pastor to perform the sermon of marriage. Paris was Georgia's maid of honour as she had no sisters of her own and her father 'Mr George Moor' and mother 'Mrs Beatrice Moor' accompanied their daughter to Jamaica for the event, so long awaited.

Rowna was looking forward to both her son's wedding and visiting her mother. She had plans of opening a care home to help children who were abandoned by their families or those who were orphans. This was something Rowna had thought of doing from a young age but now this dream could transform into reality as she was financially able to do so. However, to do this she had to do some research and make enquiries as to the feasibility of the project and location. Her intention was to stay behind after the wedding to set the plan in motion.

The Air Canada flight from Toronto flew directly to

Sangster International Airport in Montego Bay with most of the first-class passengers being friends and family who were attending Jovan's wedding. It was raining all day but the forecast for the wedding, which was to take place in three days, was sunny and dry. All was going according to plan. Annette was not able to meet them at the airport but she was at home waiting patiently and had prepared a feast for Rowna, Bill and the grandchildren. Georgia was to arrive a day later as she had to get a replacement doctor to fill in for her whilst she was on vacation.

As expected Grandma Annette had fried fish, lobster, curried goat, fried chicken, rice and peas and tropical fruit juices prepared like she always did. She insisted that everyone had a belly full and after that they had lots of time to catch up with the gossip and the wedding plans now in motion.

Paris made sure to quiz her grandmother about the history of Jamaica and ask questions about her Great-grandmother Pearle and other members of the family. She was quite an inquisitive child but Grandma Annette loved her even more for her attributes.

The following day Georgia arrived at Norman Manley Airport in Kingston as the airport was closer to Grandma Annette's home, so Jovan went to pick her up. As the tradition for weddings required that the bride-to-be was not to see the bridegroom for at least 24 hours before the wedding, that evening he drove her back to the Moon Palace Hotel in Ochio Rios where she had reserved a luxury suite with her parents.

The next day, Rowna, Georgia and Mrs Moore went to view the hall, the cake and rehearse for the wedding as the event was to take place the following day which was Saturday, and they wanted to make sure all went smoothly. The setting was even more beautiful than Georgia could hope for and the horse-drawn carriage was perfect for the occasion. The hall that the reception was booked for overlooked the sea and the local Pentecostal church was close to the hall where the couple were to get married.

Georgia's wedding dress was made with white lace, displayed off the shoulder, and decorated with diamond on the upper half of the dress, which was knee length with a long white trail, and a diamond necklace with matching tiara. She looked stunning. Her maid of honour, Paris, wore yellow and cream and so did the page boys and flowers girls. Three of Georgia's childhood friends were also her bridesmaids and their dresses were white and peach.

Jovan got to the church an hour early to ensure he was not held up by traffic as the road conditions are unpredictable when journeying from Kingston to Mandeville especially on the weekends. He was handsomely dressed in a cream suit, traditional style, and was well shaven with a faded haircut. He looked the most handsome of all the men who attended. Georgia was late, as you can imagine; she spent all morning being adorned, her facial, her fairytale hairdo, her makeup professionally applied and all the trimmings that went with it.

The white, horse-drawn, oval-shaped carriage arrived with white horses pulling it and was beautifully decorated with yellow and white ribbons all over. Passers-by gazed on at the wedding as her carriage approached the church; she was headline news in the Gleaner (newspaper) the next day. Her glass slippers were glistening as she left the carriage and entered the church because the sun was shining brightly. Her bridesmaids, flower girls, page boys, and maid of honour were all waiting at the entrance for her and as she walked towards them the traditional music Here Comes The Bride started to play. Mr Moore held his daughter's hands delicately and walked her towards the altar where Jovan was patiently waiting.

The wedding went beautifully as planned, until a man entered the church, well dressed and was the duplicate of Jovan but older. He sat at the back of the church quietly. Rowna recognised that it was Jovan's biological father, so beckoned to the pastor to continue the ceremony as he was interrupted for a moment. Rowna rendered a song as this was written in the programme and the choir sang beautifully.

At the end, Jeff went to greet the bride and groom and gave them his blessings; he greeted Rowna and Bill and the bride's parents. He made no mention of the fact that he did not receive a formal invitation as he knew that he was an absent parent who did not make the effort to get involved in his son's life whereby the relationship between them became estranged. Jeff's intention was not to cause any fuss but just to be present for a special event in his son's life.

Jovan out of courtesy invited his father back to the hall for the reception party which he gladly accepted. The evening went well and the couple danced the night away. All their family and friends enjoyed the three-course meal and the rum cake and all the trimmings and to top it off the adults were served the Jamaican white rum punch at the end to ensure they certainly enjoyed the night.

Jovan and Georgia's planned honeymoon was in Venice, so they flew out the following day as Mr and Mrs Pritchard for the two-week luxury vacation. Rowna and Paris saw them off at the airport as the flight was quite early in the morning and most of the guests were still asleep in their hotel beds.

Rowna, accompanied by her daughter drove back to a plot of land in Mandeville that she was to view that morning. Her intention was to buy five acres of land to build the children's home. That way she was able to get involved with the designs by having the plan drawn up and sourcing the work to reputable contractors so as to be sure to get exactly what she wanted. The estate agents were waiting near the site where she intended to buy the land and at the end of the meeting an agreement was made pending the terms of contract were as agreed. Bill had business association in Jamaica and so it was not a problem to get the work started as a matter of importance. All contracts were signed and agreed before

Rowna left to return to Toronto. Grandma Annette sobbed endlessly as her daughter and grandchild left to return home. What Rowna did not realise is that this was the very last time she was going to see her mother alive.

Rowna and Bill left for the airport, being the last of those who travelled to attend the wedding to return home. Their time spent in Jamaica was great but Paris had grown homesick and was looking forward to returning home where her friends were waiting for their gifts that she promised them. The Air Canada nonstop flight took off on time heading for Toronto. "Here we come!" shouted Paris to the flight attendant as she grinned.

Chapter 16

Mysterious Visitor

The front door buzzer went off and the maid answered as normal but the voice was not one that she recognised and she was not informed by either Rowna or Bill to expect visitors that day. "Good morning, it is Yvette; can I speak to Jovan?" said the stranger.

The maid replied, "He is not in the country presently as he is on his honeymoon."

The visitor answered in a surprised manner, "What! when will he be back?"

The maid explained that she was not sure but asked if she would call back after 6pm when Rowna and Bill would be back home from work and they would be able to answer her questions. The visitor left with the intention of calling back that evening.

When Rowna returned the maid told her that they had a visitor who said she would return that evening as she needed to speak urgently with Jovan but since he was away, she would like to speak to his parents instead. Yvette did show up after 6pm that day and Rowna welcomed her as she thought it may have been a friend of her son. Yvette looked about 25 and was well dressed, looking like a professional model, but Rowna could not help but notice the bulge protruding from her stomach which was slightly disguised by the baggy dress she was wearing. Rowna welcomed her into their home and she offered her a drink and a light snack which the maid quickly prepared and served.

Yvette looked a bit troubled and tried her best to get comfortable but as Rowna feared, reading Yvette's signals, the news was not quite what she wanted to hear. Yes, Yvette was pregnant and claimed that Jovan was the father. She told Rowna that she did not know about Georgia and when she heard from a friend that Jovan was getting married a few days ago, she did not believe it, however she said Jovan was not answering his phone when she tried calling and so she thought the best thing to do was to visit. Though Rowna was in shock, being a barrister she knew it was best not to make judgements before first investigating the matter. Yvette was in tears so Rowna tried to exchange some comforting and encouraging words. Rowna paid for a cab to take Yvette home and told her that she would be in touch with her as soon as she had the chance to speak with Jovan.

Bill was home late that evening and so Rowna waited up for him because she had to speak to someone about it and did not want to ring Jovan on his honeymoon, as she could not be sure this was true, plus it was not her intention to cause trouble in her son's marriage before it even really began. Bill got in 10pm that evening and Rowna engaged him in conversation straight away as she could hold it no longer. Bill's jaw dropped; he was in disbelief and once he got his breath back he told Rowna that the matter had to be treated sensitively and he would speak to Jovan 'man to man' without involving Georgia at first instance. Rowna agreed as that was the only thing they felt was honourable to do.

Jovan returned five days later, but to his own home with

his new wife. He looked happy and well rested and the couple looked so in love and as though they were made for each other. Bill felt quite saddened as he knew the subject he had to discuss with his son was not one he particularly welcomed but there was no other solution. Bill arranged for a bar visit with Jovan a week later and they met up after work in the evening. Jovan could sense that Bill was concerned about something because he seemed tense and then Bill suddenly came out with it. "Is Yvette carrying your unborn child?"

Jovan's countenance changed and he asked Bill, "Who told you such nonsense?"

Bill explained Yvette's visit and at that moment Jovan admitted to Bill that he had a fling with her that lasted for six months but once he got engaged to Georgia he ended the relationship though they kept in touch by phone. He did not tell her about his upcoming wedding but she knew the relationship was over. He told Bill he had no idea of her pregnancy as she did not tell him.

Bill asked him what he was going to do about the situation and Jovan promised to get in touch with Yvette and discuss the matter with her. The following day as promised Jovan rang Yvette and after much discussion she told him that she was seven months pregnant and she was going to keep the baby but she felt it was best since he was now married that he had no contact with the child and it was going to be better for all involved if Georgia was not told, as she was innocent and this could only hurt her and cause problems in their marriage. Both agreed but Jovan had no intention of running away from his financial responsibility so he agreed to help her with relocation costs and monthly child maintenance. Yvette agreed and Jovan kept his word.

Rowna rang Jovan to find out what was agreed between them both and when he told her of the agreement, she was not totally happy as she felt that her first grandchild was going to be a secret and she would have no contact, however, she loved Georgia, her daughter-in-law, and knew this would hurt her deeply and so she knew she had no choice but to abide by Jovan's decision. She did ask Jovan to make sure he did not just totally give up all rights to the child legally and that he try to visit at least yearly so that the child could know him. Rowna and Bill did not tell Paris as they knew it was too much to ask her to keep such a secret and her curious nature would overwhelm her and the secret would be no more.

Rowna did confide in her own mother Annette as it was important that she knew she had a great-grandchild born to her grandson. She was not happy with the family secret but she understood why it was best for all concerned.

Two months later a baby girl was born to Yvette and Jovan. She was named by her mother 'Jovannah'. Annette and Rowna were given photos of the child who Rowna vouched resembled Jovan as a baby. A DNA test was carried out just to ensure the child belonged to Jovan and Yvette made no fuss and remained in the background for many years, hence the family secret stayed a secret for some time.

Chapter 17

Georgia's Disappointment

Jovan and Georgia had been trying for a baby for a couple of years with no luck. Georgia had medical issues that were dampening the possibility of pregnancy for the couple. Georgia being a doctor herself knew that there were complications due to her having an abortion in her early teenage years. She tried fertility treatment such as IUI and IVF, surgical procedures and medicines. The couple had started to give up hope in having their own child so they started to contemplate surrogacy, which Jovan was not entirely in favour of but as he loved Georgia he was willing to go along with the plan to keep her happy.

Jovan longed to tell Georgia about Jovannah but knew that it would make the situation worse and so it was not an option. They signed up to an agency for surrogacy and had a six-month waiting period but time passed very quickly as they had busy lives. The surrogate mother (Phoebe) was Canadian and she had children of her own and so this was comforting to Jovan and Georgia because that would at least indicate that she could carry the baby full term and would be willing to hand the baby over at the end as she already had children of her own.

The cost of surrogacy varied greatly as no pregnancy can be predicted to go as planned and sometimes complications can develop whereby expenses could become costly, including doctor bills etc. A realistic cost would be starting from $60,000 onwards and could rise to $100,000. The traditional method of surrogacy was chosen by the parties where Phoebe's eggs would be inseminated with Jovan's sperm as Georgia was unable to use her own.

Due to the rigidity of Canadian law regarding surrogacy, Georgia and Jovan hired the service of a qualified fertility lawyer. This is because the law in Canada states that it is illegal to pay a surrogate mother for her services, however, it is legal to reimburse her for her reasonable expenses incurred as a result of the surrogacy. The law that governs surrogacy there is called 'The Assisted Human Reproduction Act' and therefore to avoid complications the earlier a fertility lawyer can be contacted once the intended parents and the surrogate mother approve of working together to produce a child, the earlier the surrogacy agreement can be drafted and negotiated, setting out the rights and legal obligations of each party.

Phoebe's pregnancy had no complications and at the end of the nine months a beautiful baby boy was born to the proud parents Georgia and Jovan. As we can imagine this child was a blessing and Phoebe had no regrets in working with Georgia and Jovan and was reimbursed for all expenses paid handsomely.

Rowna was ecstatic about the grandchild whom she longed for. Baby Luke was spoilt in many ways as Grandma Rowna constantly bombarded him with gifts and cuddles. Great-Grandma Annette was unable to travel due to her arthritis and other medical complications but she kept in touch by regular phone calls and Skype.

Paris was excited, believing that Baby Luke was her

brother's first child, but yes, this was her first nephew. Jovan felt guilty because he was not able to honour his role as a dedicated father to Jovannah and he was unable to share the knowledge with her about her brother Luke. Georgia was very happy indeed because now she was a mother which she had longed for.

Sadly shortly after the birth, the news which Rowna feared most arrived; Annette had died which was unexpected. She was ill, yes, with rheumatoid arthritis and high blood pressure, but she was taking regular medication. Rowna had to book an emergency flight to Jamaica and the family joined her later.

Grandma Annette was buried in a tomb close to her mother and father and after the reading of Annette's will, Rowna left the property with an estate agent for rental and she also visited the children's home and gave some provisions she brought for them.

For some time after the funeral Annette went into a state of depression and she was unable to eat well. However, after medical assistance she recovered and returned to work soon after. Rowna had lost her mother for the second time but this time it was permanent.

Chapter 18

Jovan Meets Danny

Jovan received a telegram from Jamaica marked urgent which Georgia collected from the hotel reception area whilst they were in Madrid, Spain, after receiving a call from the hotel management. They had left Baby Luke with Rowna for a weekend break.

The telegram was addressed to Jovan and read: 'call Danny as soon as you receive this message urgently.' The only Danny Jovan could recall from Jamaica was his half-brother, his father's son, and he wondered what was the urgency. He immediately rang the number on the telegram and Danny answered the phone. He said, "Dad is in hospital and he is not expected to live much longer because he had a major stroke and has lost consciousness." Jovan was mystified. He tried to say comforting words and assured Danny that he would be there by the end of the week. When Jovan put the phone down he explained to Georgia that he had to book a flight to Jamaica once he got back home and he also rang his mum to inform her of what Danny told him.

Jovan felt downhearted because he had really started

getting to know his father after seeing him at his wedding; they kept in contact with each other. He landed in Kingston Norman Manley Airport within a few days and Danny picked him up from the airport. They drove to the University College Hospital in Kingston where Jeff was admitted and he was still unconscious. He was hooked up to several different life support machines and Jovan walked over to him, sat down beside his bed and held his hand. The room was dimly lit with the sunshine peeping through the blinds which were slightly opened, and silence shadowed the room as though time stood still.

Dad looked peacefully, as though he was sleeping normally, but when Jovan tried whispering into his ears, "Dad it's me, Jovan, I am here," there was silence and no reply. Danny glanced over at Jovan, shaking his head and tears running down his cheeks. At that moment Jeff slightly opened his eyes and Jovan called for the doctor who was responsible for his father's care. Jovan told him his dad had opened his eyes and at that point Jeff opened his eyes but looked confused. The doctor asked them to leave the room whilst he carried out some checks and he asked them to wait in the waiting area where he would later assist them.

Half an hour later the doctor walked into the waiting room and asked both brothers to step inside his consultation room where he had good news, explaining that their dad had regained consciousness but it was too early to say if any damage had been done to his brain as they needed tests to be carried out to determine that. Though the hospital had a good reputation Jovan was taking no chances with Jeff's recovery so he rang Bill and asked for his advice. Bill was thankfully able to get Jeff admitted to a private hospital which would guarantee premium medical attention and treatment.

Jovan spoke to Danny and Jeff's wife regarding transferring him and they both agreed without any disputes or contention so Jeff was transported by ambulance the same evening. Jeff recovered from his stroke though his speech was affected somewhat.

Over the next two weeks Jovan stayed in a nearby hotel but visited his father daily where he was able to see Danny, who never left Jeff's side throughout his illness. During this time the two brothers got to know each other quite well; they realised they had a lot in common and were both ambitious.

Jovan realise that Danny was in the army and had now applied to NASA for an astronaut position. He was quite impressed when Danny told him that he had a bachelor's degree in engineering and a masters in mathematics. He had more than 1,000 hours of pilot-in-command time in jet aircraft. He was being sponsored by the government. Danny explained that if he got accepted, taking into account many other skills that he possessed whilst training in the military, such as gaining another language (Russian), qualified scuba diver, military water survival training and more, he would be transferred overseas for a period of five years for training in total.

Danny had high hopes and explained to Jovan that as a boy he wanted to become an astronaut, so he studied hard and after graduating from university, he joined the military but because he had achieved a scholarship to attend due to his excellent grades, the government funded his education programme. However, he explained to Jovan that he had been turned down twice before by NASA but he was determined to pursue his ultimate ambition. Jovan knew that Danny had no intention of giving up with the passionate tone he used when he spoke. He was one day going to enrol unto the two-years training for the International Space Station. He was also aware that there were international partners with training facilities in Canada and that would be an opportunity for Danny to spend some time with him and his family.

Jeff was recovering though was physically weak with slight speech impairment but regardless of his illness he was happy to see his sons bonding together and knew that this was the beginning of a great relationship.

Jovan went to view the children's home which was inhabited by over 30 children. The staff were very accommodating and he approved of the way the home was facilitated and operated. He was able to report back to Rowna of their good conduct and the wellbeing of the children.

Georgia and Baby Luke drove to the airport to collect Jovan as he could not wait to see them both and neither could they wait to see him. Well, he had lots to share with them about his trip and that Baby Luke had an uncle that he was yet to meet.

Chapter 19

Bill's Family Reunion – the Secret

Revealed

The family reunion was once again being celebrated but this time in Toronto. Bill was to host the venue as the baton was passed to him after his father's death to carry on the family tradition.

The guest list was growing over time because the younger generation was multiplying in numbers. Rowna under Bill's instruction sent out the invitations to all the family three weeks in advance. The press was interested in this particular event because it was the 50th reunion celebrated over the years.

The headlines in the local papers read 'Upcoming 50th reunion of the Diego Family to be held in Toronto this month'.

Two weeks before the celebration Jovan visited Jovannah, who was now age seven. Her mother had finally agreed for visitation twice each year for the benefit of her daughter having a relationship with her biological father. As well as the visits Jovan could speak to his daughter via phone calls. Unknown to him, a news reporter got hold of the story about the family secret from an unknown source and he began to investigate the tip-off in the hope of unveiling that Jovan had a lovechild outside of his marriage.

Jovan took his daughter to a restaurant for lunch and then to the cinema and they had great fun. At the end of the day he took Jovannah back home to her mother and started his journey home.

The following morning the headlines in The Globe and Mail newspapers read 'The Secret Child of Jovan; meet Jovannah day out with dad'. There was a picture with Jovan and Jovannah outside the cinema. Rowna rang Jovan on his mobile and enquired whether he had seen the papers, but as it was quite early in the morning he had not had the chance to collect his newspaper from his front lawn where the paperboy usually throws it on his delivery rounds each morning. She warned her son to get the paper before Georgia did because he needed to see the headline urgently. She hung up and Jovan quickly went to get the paper as Georgia was still in the bathroom getting ready for work.

Jovan curiously looked at the headlines, seeing a picture of him and Jovannah which must have been taken the day before. He was confused but realised that the secret was out now and he had no time to make enquiries as to how the leak came about and how the reporter was able to get hold of his well-kept secret. Jovan paced up and down the bedroom breaking out in a cold sweats as he had no choice but to quickly tell Georgia before anyone else informed her or worse still, she saw the headlines in the newspaper. His imagination ran wild for a moment as he felt this was sure to end up in divorce, which is why he didn't tell her in the first place. He could not help but feel sorry for himself and he could not bear the thought of losing Luke also.

Jovan drank two glasses of whisky within a short period of

time to help him settle his nerve and sat himself down on the bed awaiting Georgia opening the bathroom door. Georgia finally opened the door with her long curly hair wrapped in a towel and a white robe around her slender body. "Honey, your turn now. Hurry, it is getting late," said Georgia. He looked a bit disturbed and so Georgia asked him what was wrong. He took her by the hand and gently sat her down on the bed next to him. He asked her to just listen without interrupting him because what he had to tell her was of importance and he wanted her to hear him out before saying anything. Georgia sat silently and listened. Jovan told Georgia the whole story and she was bemused at what she was hearing. With tears in her eyes she asked her husband who else knew. He told her his parents and the late Grandma Annette.

Georgia cried and Jovan could not console her, then she kept silent and refused to exchange another word with him before she hurriedly got dressed and left for work.

Jovan knew in his heart that this was going to be a challenging and trying time in their marriage and he could not fix it with any amount of money, he was just going to have to exercise patience and pray that Georgia would forgive him. Jovan rang his mother and they discussed the issue and she encouraged him to give Georgia space and time and assured him that his wife was wise and would not make any rash decision, but he also had to do whatever it took to make it up to her and walk on eggshells. However, they both agreed that it was a relief that the secret was a secret no more and that Georgia finally knew of Jovannah.

Georgia rang Rowna later that day and after floods of tears shed between both women the story that Jovan told his wife was confirmed by Rowna and so though Georgia was deeply hurt she understood why the story was kept a secret, and also that Jovan was not to blamed because he did not know of the pregnancy until after the wedding. Being a doctor who herself had an abortion in her teenage years and the consequences she suffered as a result, helped her understood that aborting the child was not the best option always and so it 'lightened the blow' somewhat.

Nevertheless, Georgia felt that Jovan should have told her sooner and that he would have kept the secret for longer if the reporter hadn't discovered the truth and published it. Georgia was as smart as Rowna sensed, but also intelligent too, after all, she had Luke to consider and knew that she was strong enough to get through this crisis as she loved her husband enough and was not prepared to give up nearly eight years of marriage. Georgia suggested to her husband to invite the child to the family reunion as she too was a Diego and had every right to be welcomed and accepted into the family.

Jovan knew at that point that he had made the right choice to marry Georgia; she sure was special and second to none. Rowna and Bill were relieved and were content to finally put this saga to rest. Rowna was ecstatic as she could now have access to Jovannah and she sure needed this as Annette was now laid to rest. She was still in mourning after losing her mother for a second time but this time permanently, so having her granddaughter around her was of vital importance.

Jovannah and Luke spent time with their dad's parents in their school holidays where they bonded together and became great friends. Jovan made sure that he spent time with his wife and children when the opportunity arose and this made him happy as he didn't want his children to be estranged from him as he was with his own father as a child. History was not going to repeat itself if he could help it.

The family reunion was celebrated as was expected; the hall was huge and the family all attended. All the family met Jovannah for the first time and some had not yet met Luke as he was only four years old. For Georgia and Jovan it brought back memories because they met at one of the family reunion celebrations and now they were back as husband and wife with a family of their own, so as you can imagine they fell in love all over again that summer.

Chapter 20

NASA, Here I Come

Danny after several attempts finally succeeded in being able to secure a place on the training programme for astronauts and after two years of study he took up voluntary work with the international partners with training facilities in Canada. "Finally I have made it to the finale! I am almost there," gloated Danny to his big brother Jovan as they conversed over the phone in one of their weekly 'chit-chats'.

"I knew you would get there one day," said Jovan, "because you have always spoken so passionately about making it to NASA no matter how long it took you; congratulations, bro."

Rowna, hearing the commotion over the phone loudspeaker hailed her congratulations and asked Danny when he was arriving in Canada as Paris was anxious to meet him and Bill was longing to share a round of beer at the pub with him. Danny told them that he was due to travel in a month's time and that he sure would visit as soon as he got settled into the accommodation which was being organised for him. Jovan and Danny said their goodbyes and hung up.

"Well, son, your brother is just as stubborn as you are when he sets his mind to achieving his goals but I can't say that is a bad thing on this occasion," said Rowna in a joyful way.

"I guess its Dad's stubbornness that rubs off on us both, but I agree, Mum, that it has certainly paid off for him." Jovan and Danny got on well together and one could even say that they were best friends.

The month went by quickly and Danny had moved into his new apartment and began working voluntarily, but his rent and expenses were taken care of by the state. He received a weekly allowance but was quite independent so he worked part-time on the weekends teaching maths to adult learners. After a few weeks Jovan arranged for his brother to visit him and his family and so made arrangements to pick him up for the weekend. Danny had the opportunity to meet Paris who was not disappointed with his personality as he was quite talkative, like she was, and 'cool'. Danny reminded her of Jovan as their personalities were similar. They had a fabulous weekend catching up on stories about Jamaica and about its beauty and tranquillity. Paris listened tentatively but really did not have a clue as to what they were going on about; after all, she was very much a Canadian and had never lived in Jamaica; she only visited to see Grandma Annette when she was still living and only for short periods of time.

"How long does it take to travel to space?" asked Luke and without giving his uncle a chance to answer that question he fired another at him. Jovannah and Luke asked Uncle Danny so many questions that he had to limit the number of questions they could ask to five each and then told them to write down any more questions they wanted answered about space and give them to their dad to post to him. Jovannah made a special visit that weekend to meet her Uncle Danny whom she had heard so much about, and knew he was involved with NASA and wanted to know all she could about it too. Luke was excited to see Jovannah, who he called 'Big Sis' as she always bossed him about.

The weekend went by very quickly and Danny had to return as he had work the very next day. Danny promised that he would visit again when he got time off which was due at Christmas.

Chapter 21

What a Palaver

As time went by Jovannah grew up into a splendid young lady and she was as ambitious as her grandmother Rowna. She formed a special bond with Rowna and she loved her endlessly. In fact Rowna saw a duplicate of herself in her granddaughter. However, there was a bit of resentment as Georgia felt that Rowna paid too much attention to Jovannah and somewhat neglected Luke. Because of this Georgia limited Jovannah's visits to twice a year but Rowna, disagreeing with this arrangement, insisted that Jovannah could visit as much as she wanted to but instead of going to stay with her dad she could stay with her. This caused conflict between Georgia and Rowna, but Rowna was not going to back down as she felt Georgia was being unreasonable to Jovannah. Jovan of course was placed in an awkward situation as he loved both his mother and his wife but he also knew his mother enough to know that she was not going to have it any other way, and she felt Yvette (Jovannah's mother) had been quite reasonable over the years, never causing a scene and always thinking about what was best for the family.

Georgia tried desperately to cause separation between Luke and Jovannah and she showed this clearly when she sent Luke to private school in Switzerland after much debate between Jovan and the rest of the family. Yvette, listening to her daughter despair in being told that her brother was going to attend boarding school in Switzerland, thought she would try to have a word with Georgia to explain how distraught Jovannah was about the matter.

Unbeknown to Jovan about Yvette's intention, she called and Georgia answered the phone. She listened to what Yvette had to say but after listening she launched a verbal attack at her, stating that it was not her business to get involved in the matter and she should stay out of it because she was an outcast and would always be seen as such within the family.

Yvette was devastated by Georgia's behaviour and rang Rowna to complain, and Rowna then intervened by calling Georgia and said to her, "How dare you call Yvette an outcast? She is the mother of my first grandchild and should be treated with respect. You are causing trouble in this family and I am warning you to stop this foolishness before I have to settle the matter; you are damn out of order and I want no more of this nonsense spoken in this family." Then she hung up the phone before Georgia could reply.

Georgia was fuming and went to the drink cabinet; she poured a stiff brandy and took a few mouthfuls before calling Jovan. Jovan could hardly hear what she was saying on his end of the phone as she was speaking in a high-pitched tone, being furious with her mother-in-law for speaking to her in a rude manner. Jovan tried to calm her down and asked her to speak at a lower tone as he could not comprehend what she was saying to him. Georgia had no intention of taking any orders or instructions from anyone so she slammed the phone on Jovan and called her best friend Juanita and explained what had just taken place. Juanita took side with Georgia and 'heaped more coal into the fire' by stating that Georgia should cut Jovan's family off from any contact with her or Luke, and that she should do what she felt was right for her son.

Jovan rang his mother to ascertain what was going on between her and his wife and when she explained he decided to ring Yvette. Yvette reiterated to Jovan what she said to Georgia and that she did not expect to get the response she received, but she also told Jovan that she was not going accept such insult from his wife and that Jovannah had always shown respect to Georgia as a stepmother, so this behaviour was unacceptable, and if the matter was not sorted out Jovannah was not going to be allowed to visit him in his marital home again. If he wanted to see her then he would have to do so at his mother's home.

Jovannah wanted no contact with Georgia as she was hurt about what she said to her mother and her behaviour towards her. Jovannah spoke with both Luke and Grandma Rowna to let them know that her love for them both was unconditional but as Georgia certainly did not like her it was best that she kept her distance; at least until the argument blew over.

Jovannah was very creative and pursued fashion and also for a short time entered a few modelling contests. She corresponded with her brother by letter and occasional phone calls whilst he was in Switzerland and she even visited him there a few times.

Once Luke finished school he returned to Canada but by then Jovannah had left to attend university in New York to complete a degree in fashion design. Georgia had formed a barrier between herself and Rowna, but Rowna was sticking to her decision; she was not going to let Georgia's stubbornness and jealousy come between her grandchildren, especially when she had it all wrong. Rowna did not love any of her grandchildren more than the other, but due to having very little access to Jovannah in her early years, she tried to compensate in some ways and Jovannah was naturally a lovely girl who was affectionate and was easily loved.

After quite a number of years had passed Georgia eventually realised her mistake in trying to separate the children and also realised that this was to no avail as they were inseparable. She eventually apologised to Rowna, Yvette and Jovannah but it was never the same again as there was 'too much water under the bridge'. However, so saying, they were humane towards each other and continued to attend the family reunions which only got bigger as the family grew yearly.

Chapter 22

Jovannah the Author

Jovannah, after successfully graduating from university returned to Canada and started a fashion line in her own company. She became a multinational millionaire, owning companies all over the world in the fashion industry. Jovannah had no time to accommodate a husband and did not marry as she was constantly travelling from one country to the other.

She took care of her biological mother and had a full time carer for her mother when she was away on business trips. Her mother, Yvette, developed dementia at age 62 and so needed full-time care as the condition got worse.

Jovannah was contacted by Yvette's neighbour when they saw smoke coming from her kitchen window after alerting the emergency fire services. The neighbours had spare house keys to the property in the case of an emergency. The neighbour rang the doorbell and when she was unable to get a reply, entered the property. Luckily for Yvette she was in the bathroom at the time which protected her from smoke inhalation but she was unaware that the pot she left on the stove for hours cooking lunch had caught fire. The neighbour helped her out of the bath, got her bathrobe on and quickly bundled her out of the house and into a safe area at the front.

The fire crew arrived within minutes and put the fire out and commended the neighbour for her brave conduct and rescuing Yvette from what could have been a fatal outcome. Yvette arrived later that afternoon as she was miles away when she received the phone call and she thanked her neighbour for saving her mother's life, and she also rewarded her handsomely for her bravery by donating a significant sum of money to her chosen charity.

Jovannah had realised that her mother's memory was not as sharp as it once was but she assumed that it was age related, however, she had no idea of the severity of the illness until she had Yvette tested and diagnosed. Jovannah was told that her mother's case fell into the 9% of cases who show onset of the disease before the age of 65. Research has shown a relationship between development of cognitive impairment in terms of physical inactivity, obesity, and unbalanced diets, use of tobacco and alcohol and midlife hypertension, with other non-communicable disease.

Yvette enjoyed tobacco and alcohol intake on a daily basis and she also was obese, so Jovannah was advised to keep a close eye on her mother's diet as well as alcohol and tobacco consumption. Though it was a struggle to convince Yvette to change her lifestyle altogether to help her health condition, she loved her daughter unconditionally and so worked with a health plan that would help her to slow down the process of the dementia and live healthily, therefore reducing the risk of additional health problems.

Jovannah's growing interest in her family history and her years of studying the family tree led her to writing this book. Spending time with Great-Grandma Annette, Grandma Rowna and her dad Jovan proved valuable, collecting the information in order to write her manuscript and finally getting her book published after many years.

She sometimes felt that though she was the illegitimate child, born at what she termed an awkward moment, she had a purpose that needed to be fulfilled because she had a father who loved her and so did not abandon her; instead he worked with her mother to make sure she lacked nothing. She had grandparents who acknowledged her and kept in touch regardless of the risk they faced. She had a mother who protected her at all cost and swallowed her pride to work with her dad's family for her sake.

Jovannah also made it a point of duty to ring her brother Luke and visit him when she could as Georgia was not always very welcoming. However, Jovan was sure to keep the communication link going with his children as he was a family man and knew they would one day inherit a great fortune, so he wanted to ensure that they would be able to manage it together as a team.

Chapter 23

Luke's Fatality

The evening was cold and cloudy as it was winter and snow was falling heavily all week. Luke was expected back from Switzerland that night from a business meeting that he had to attend as he was managing director of his dad's international engineering company. He was picked up by his driver from the airport and so Bill and Rowna were expecting him for dinner. "I wonder what's taking Luke so long; surely he should have been back by now," said Bill to Rowna. Rowna continued preparing the potato salad; as dinner was running late anyway she was happy he was late which gave her enough time to finish. Another couple of hours went by and Luke still did not arrive. Rowna decided to ring as she felt he may have stopped off somewhere forgetting he had dinner plans. She dialled his number and got no reply and also his chauffeur and had no response from him either.

Rowna's mobile phone rang just as she was about to call Jovan; Georgia was on the other end and sounded as though she had something stuck in her throat as she could hardly speak. She told her that Luke had been in a car accident and was brought in by an air ambulance; he was being operated on in the emergency room and they should come immediately. Rowna in a panic said to Bill, "We have to go now." Bill had overheard the conversation between his wife and Georgia so he grabbed his jacket and car keys and headed for the door.

Bill and Rowna got to the hospital within half an hour as it was late evening and the roads weren't busy. When they got to the emergency entrance Georgia was there to meet them and she told them that Jovan was on his way. They tried to enquire about what went wrong but Georgia was unable to shed any light on the situation, however, the police arrived shortly after who explained to them that the matter was being investigated and they would be notified as soon as information became available. Bill and Rowna waited for two hours with Georgia and they waited for Jovan to arrive. Georgia told them that the chauffeur did not make it as he died at the scene.

The night was long and the wait was agonising and Jovan finally arrived to help console his wife, Georgia, who was devastated but tried to remain strong for her family. Doctor Moore who was the operating surgeon slowly came walking towards Georgia and Jovan with great sadness displayed on his pale face after working for hours trying to resuscitate Luke. He asked both parents and grandparents to join him in a private area and gently broke the news to them, assuring them that he did all he could but Luke had sustained multiple injuries and was not responding to treatment. He was pronounced dead at 10:07pm. Georgia broke down and had to be sedated as she suffered from high blood pressure. Jovan, Rowna and Bill were upset but had to try to remain calm for Georgia's sake.

The next day the police visited Jovan's home where Rowna and Bill were staying in order to help with the arrangements that had to be made for Luke's funeral and also to give support to their son and his family. The investigation revealed that the chauffeur was on his way with Luke to Rowna's home when there was a police chase in progress and the car that was being chased hit their car and it turned over, rolling several times before coming to a halt. The driver was thrown from the car and died instantly whilst Luke had to be cut out of his seat. He was still alive when was brought to casualty but later died from multiple head and chest injuries.

The driver in the other car was injured but survived and therefore would be charged with both deaths and reckless driving. This was a police matter and so would be dealt with by the state.

Jovannah and Paris came as soon as they heard the news. Jovannah was very close to Luke and had only just spoken to him whilst he was on his trip in Switzerland three days before the accident. She was bereaved with disbelief, unable to digest that her younger brother was killed so tragically. The news made headlines in most major papers in Canada. Luke was well loved by many of his extended family and was family orientated, so for this reason his funeral was expected to be attended by over 500 people including his friends, work colleagues and family.

The flowers and cards arriving daily after his death were endless. Some of the flowers had to be donated to charity and to the hospital where he took his last breath. Georgia was in no fit state to make the funeral arrangements so Rowna, Danny and Bill made most of the necessary arrangements with friends and staff helping out. Luke's body was churched at St James' Cathedral and he was laid to rest in a private burial plot in Toronto. Sadly Luke will be missed by all as his death was untimely and sudden.

Chapter 24

Danny the Astronaut Finds Happiness

Danny finished his training as an astronaut and started working for NASA. He lived in Washington DC, but would travel to Canada twice each year to see Jovan and family. During his travels to Canada he met an African-American lady, who was a practicing solicitor, on one of his flights. They maintained a long-distance relationship for a period of time until they decided to commit to each other by getting married and they both moved to Washington DC as Danny worked at NASA's headquarters.

The wedding took place in Canada as his wife's family lived there and also his family so it was convenient for the wedding to be held there. A year after their wedding, his wife, Althea, fell pregnant and gave birth to triplet girls. This was a blessing to the family as there was no history in either family of triplets.

Rowna and Bill were godparents to the girls and of course after losing their grandson it was an honour though in no way a replacement. Danny took the children and his new wife to meet his mother and father in Jamaica. They gave them a surprise as Jovan visited too. Jeff and Shelley were overjoyed to see them and to know that there was unity within their family, as well as how ambitious and successful their adult children were, plus having a big family. Jeff, however, was still in mourning because of his grandson whom he had outlived and the sadness that remained with Jovan for the loss of his beloved son.

Chapter 25

Goodbye Jeff

Jeff changed over the years and finally settled with Shelley, whom he loved. He had a stroke but with a change of lifestyle and healthy living he lived for many years and was able to enjoy his sons and grandchildren's visits. Jeff never travelled to Canada because of ill health. His sons invited him on numerous occasions but he refused the offers and his wife Shelley would not travel without her husband, due to his medical condition. The triplets kept them busy when they visited and Danny and Jovan would try to plan their visits to Jamaica together so that the children could keep in touch with each other and enjoy the family reunion. This was done twice each year.

Jeff at age 72 had a heart attack and at the time his family was visiting from Canada and Washington DC. He was in hospital for a few days when they found a blockage in an artery. A week later he had a second heart attack which was major and as a result he died.

The funeral arrangement was made over a short period of time, but as Jeff's family had their own burial plot, it made it easier for the family to organise the funeral and most of Shelley and Jeff's families resided in Jamaica, so they only had to await the arrival of Rowna, Jovannah and Paris.

Rowna over the years had kept in touch with Jeff after Jovannah's secret birth came out into the open. They buried the hatchet and developed a great friendship as they had a child and grandchildren whom they both shared. In fact he was finding it hard to come to terms with the loss of his grandson Luke. He had a close relationship with Luke because he was the type of grandson who made it a regular occurrence to ring his granddad and have a chat. He kept Jeff informed with everyone's wellbeing and so Jeff was heartbroken when he heard his favourite grandson had died so suddenly.

Rowna, her daughter and granddaughter stayed at her house in Kingston which Grandma Pearle left her, and they visited Grandma Pearle's grave and laid flowers as a sign of respect. Also Rowna was able to share her childhood memories with the girls. Jovannah was able to record some of the information for her memoirs.

Jeff's body was churched in the local Catholic church in Kingston, the parish in which he was born, and he was buried in Montego Bay where his grandparents and their decedents originated from.

After the funeral Rowna and her family visited the orphanage that she built and managed. Paris and Jovannah were fascinated with the children who lived there and the staff who took care of them. They realised how fortunate they were living in Canada and having everything they needed at their disposal.

Rowna, now getting on in age, knew she had to pass on the responsibilities of management of the orphanage to one of her offspring. Jovan was always busy with his own company and soon he would have to take on the role of Chairman to Bill's company as he was soon to retire. During their visits whilst in Jamaica Rowna discussed the opportunity with Paris and Jovannah; they agreed to jointly manage the orphanage and felt that it would be more beneficial to do so. This was a relief to Rowna as she was growing old and wanted to cut down on her travelling commitments.

Shelley was very stubborn and set in her ways and so refused to move to Washington DC with her son Danny. She felt she was too old to live anywhere else except Jamaica and she wanted to be buried beside her husband when she was finally laid to rest. They all knew it was pointless arguing with her and so they got her a live-in carer who would take care of her daily needs and her home. Shelley though reluctant agreed to that.

Danny and Jovan visited twice yearly to see Shelley until she eventually died of old age at 82. As she requested, they buried her beside her husband in Montego Bay.

Chapter 26

Paris Reveals All

Paris's first love was a young man named James. They met whilst she was on holiday in Hawaii. They met at a club in Honolulu and continued a long-distance relationship for almost a year. The relationship came to an end when James met someone else who lived in Hawaii. Paris was upset but came to terms with the fact that things weren't working out due to their commitments at university as well as the long distance.

Paris later met Tegan who was a typical playboy. Paris soon realised this when she discovered his second mobile phone hidden in his car glove compartment whilst she was waiting as he went to pay the cashier for the fuel at the petrol station. The phone rang and Paris followed the sound of the ring tone which led to the glove compartment; she took the phone out with the intention of taking it over to Tegan who was waiting in the queue, but at that point it stopped ringing, and that was followed by a text which read, 'Hi stud, missing you terribly; have you booked the hotel room for tonight?'

Paris decided to respond so she typed, 'where did you

have in mind darling?'

And the response via text was: 'the Hiltons of course; hope you have booked in advance as you promised'.

Paris replied via text, 'sure sweetheart, see you later'. She quickly deleted the text messages so as to erase any evidence or suspicions. She then placed the phone back.

When Tegan got back to the car, she asked him what he was doing over the weekend as it was Friday. On occasion he would go off with his friends over the weekend, at least that is what he told her and what she believed. He pretended to have forgotten to mention that he would be going away with his friends that night in his reply to her and said he would be back Sunday evening. Paris played along with his game and asked where he would be going. He told her nothing about the hotel plans and gave her a made-up story. She said nothing to give him any indication of what she now knew. That evening Paris called a girlfriend over who drove her to the Hiltons where she patiently waited for the arrival of Tegan and the mystery lady.

As expected Tegan drove up in his black BMW sports car and parked in the nearby car park. He got out of the car with a blonde, slender-looking chick and they both got their cases out of the back of the car and proceeded towards the Hilton hotel entrance. Paris hid behind a few cars and took photographs of them, including ones where they were kissing and caressing each other. She then got back into the car and phoned his mobile. He stopped, looked at the phone and put it back in his pocket. He did not answer the call. Paris left with her friend who dropped her back home where she cried and told her mother what she had just experienced. She showed her mother the photos she had taken of them and Rowna desperately tried to console her and did her best to cheer Paris up.

Rowna asked her what she was going to do about the situation. Rowna also advised that she could give him the chance to explain before making a decision. Paris felt she had enough evidence to determine what she was going to do and though she would give him a chance to explain, the trust was already broken as he lied to her, telling her that he was going away with his friends, and the question that most bothered Paris was how long had this been going on and how serious was the relationship between him and the blonde?

Tegan did return her call later that night, possibly when his friend was asleep and continued the lies, trying to explain why he was unable to answer her call earlier that day. Paris did not tell him anything, instead she waited for Sunday when he returned and visited her. She let him talk about his imaginary weekend away first and then she presented him with the photos. He almost fell over when Paris handed them to him. There was nothing he could have said in his defence except that he was sorry. Paris looked at him with pity and told him that she would not be seeing him anymore.

He tried his best to win her back for weeks after that but Paris's heart was broken and she was not prepared to venture into such a dishonest and make-believe relationship again. Tegan and Paris remained acquaintances but the romance was over.

Paris stayed single for a year or so before she met her true love but no one knew who it was until she came out in public, admitting that she was in a lesbian relationship and she was to marry her girlfriend Olivia. Rowna found it hard to accept that her daughter was gay and as a result refused to welcome Olivia in their home. Bill tried to encourage Rowna to meet with Olivia so that she could get to know her personally but Rowna was not easily persuaded.

This made Paris and her mother's relationship estranged somewhat. Rowna could not accept the fact that her only daughter was gay and Paris was not going to try to live her life to please her mum.

Jovan loved his sister enough to accept her for who she

was even though he could not understand why she preferred having an intimate relationship with a female rather than a male. Georgia and Jovan invited the couple for dinner so that they could meet with Olivia and get to know her better. Paris shared her concerns about Rowna refusing to meet with Olivia and declaring that she would not be attending the wedding.

Olivia was originally from Barcelona, but her family migrated to Canada when she was an infant. She went to public schools and was of a middle-class background. Olivia's parents were accepting of both their daughter's and Paris's relationship and gave them their blessings when they notified them of their intentions for marriage.

Rowna did not have any animosity towards Olivia as a person but she just could not accept the relationship.

Paris was determined to share her life with her partner and to seal their commitment they got married in Toronto, though not in a church. They chose to marry in a registry office and only close family and friends were invited as they preferred a private wedding. Rowna reluctantly attended and Bill gave his daughter's hand in marriage. Bill, Jovan, Georgia, Jovannah, Danny and his family were all present and of course Olivia's family.

Eventually Rowna accepted that her daughter had to make her own choice in deciding whom she married and as she loved her daughter, they were invited to all family reunions and the occasional family gatherings.

Chapter 27

Georgia Undergoes a Mental Breakdown

Georgia worked for many years in her own private clinic but as she got on in age she decided to practice medicine on a smaller scale, so she worked part-time a few days per week at the local hospital and sold on her private clinic. She finally made the decision after Luke's death as she was finding it hard to cope with her loss. Georgia had seemed to somewhat distance herself at times from the rest of the family but that was expected as she was a quiet person anyway.

Georgia spent most evenings after Luke's burial at the cemetery, cleaning the tomb and replacing flowers. She would make a list of the things she still wanted to say to Luke which she did not get the chance to do as his passing was so soon. She would cry whilst she spoke the words from her list, in desperate hope that somehow he would be able to hear her. One day when she was visiting Luke she met a lady who was also visiting a grave in the same cemetery and they got talking and she poured her heart out to this woman, telling her of her despair at her child being taken from her so suddenly without

"

her being able to say goodbye. The lady gave her the phone number of a spiritualist who would be able to help her contact her son in the spirit world.

Georgia, being vulnerable and in despair called the woman and arranged to meet and discussed her sorrows. Georgia, after visiting several times was besotted with the results as she was led to believe that Luke was present on occasion and was able to communicate with her through performing various rituals. Georgia finally came to her senses when she saw the strings attached to the curtains that were being drawn by a childlike figure whose reflection she saw in a nearby glass cabinet as she pulled the strings.

Georgia got up from the table she was sitting at and flung open the front door and ran non-stop until she got home. She then began to withdraw slowly into a world of her own.

Jovan began to notice that she would at times lock herself away in her bedroom and would refuse to get dressed unless prompted to if she was not going to work. Some days she would neglect going to work and when Jovan enquired she said she forgot what day it was. It was becoming very clear to see that Georgia was not herself. After much debate Georgia agreed to see a psychiatrist of her choice because she knew she needed help and it was not just grief. The psychiatrist diagnosed Georgia with depression and prescribed medication to help the condition.

Georgia failed to take her medication most days and so the condition worsened. Jovan, being concerned, asked his mum to visit Georgia daily to check on her as he was quite aware that this blow was more than she could bear. Rowna, now working from home in an office built into the side of their family home, was able to visit her daily and would help her get dressed and comb her hair.

Georgia was never the same again and at times she would just go off on her own without notifying Jovan of her whereabouts, but after a few days would return home. She refused to part with Luke's belongings which Jovan and Paris would try to encourage her to do, believing that it would help her.

One spring day when it was raining Georgia decided that she could no longer go on with the grief she was enduring so she took a bottle of pills and Rowna found her outside in the garden underneath the apple tree with the rain beating down on her drenched body, laying still. She called for an ambulance and called Jovan who made his way to the hospital. Rowna drove behind the ambulance and remained by her side until her son got there.

The doctors managed to pump the tablets from her stomach and she regained consciousness but they warned that she was lucky that Rowna had found her because otherwise she would not have survived. After that episode Rowna had Georgia stay with her for a few months until she was well enough to return to work.

Georgia and Jovan decided to move house in order to give them a fresh start whereby the memories of Luke would not be so profound. Georgia in time learned to accept Luke's death though not fully getting over it, as a parent does not plan to outlive their child.

Chapter 28

The Retirement Party

Bill and Rowna were now pensioners and together made the decision to retire. They had worked very hard in their adult lives and felt it was time to spend more time together visiting those places that they had vowed to visit before they departed from this life. To celebrate their retirement they decided to throw a party and invite close friends, work colleagues and all members of their family and extended family.

The event was to be held at The Symes in Toronto. The cost per guest was $300. The invitations were sent out a month before the event to ensure that the majority could attend. In total 500 guests were expected to attend the party. Bill and Rowna were busy trying to make the arrangements with the children helping out when they could.

Lucy flew over from New York to help her best friend prepare for the big event and surprisingly she took her partner Leonard along who appeared to be a gentleman indeed. Lucy did not seem very happy in her persona even though she was trying to disguise it with her plastic smile, but as soon as an opportunity arose for Rowna to sneak Lucy out of the house to make an errand to the shop, she did so. Once they were in the car Rowna asked her friend what was bothering her as it was obvious to her that something wasn't right. Lucy was a bit reluctant to disclose what was on her mind as the occasion she was there for was a happy one, so she did not feel it was the appropriate time.

Rowna, not letting up, insisted that she spoke with her in confidence, so Lucy told her that Leonard had asked her to marry him and though she was flattered and was happy he finally asked for her hand in marriage, she could not accept due to the fact that he had a child with another woman whom he was having an affair with for a short time. Lucy told her that the little boy resembled him and he accepted responsibility by giving monthly child maintenance and went to see the child every two weeks. However, she still loved him, but was not ready for marriage especially whilst feeling such betrayal and hurt over the matter. Tears fell down her cheeks as she poured out her heart to Rowna, who hugged her and tried her best to comfort her friend.

Rowna knew what betrayal felt like as she went through a similar incident with her ex-husband Jeff. All she could advise her friend was to give it time as she needed to heal. This was a matter of the heart so could not be rushed but in time she would learn to forgive Leonard as he did admit his wrong, ended the relationship and remained with no intention of leaving. Rowna knew she could not mend Lucy's heart, but she also knew that Lucy would make the right decision eventually because she was of strong character and usually made the right decisions in the end.

Rowna was determined to at least help take Lucy's mind off her problems whilst she was staying with her and that she did, because they were busy making plans and preparations for the retirement party. Lucy, being in the hospitality industry, had a lot of input and was able to help with choosing the best caterers who were accredited for their outstanding service. The choice of colours had to be determined and this was not an easy subject as Rowna and Lucy could not quite agree on the same colours, but in the end they compromised; Rowna decided on the women's dress code and Lucy on the men's.

The men's dress code was tuxedos with white silk shirt and gold ties and the ladies had to wear black and gold evening gowns. The male guests were required to wear black dress shoes and females were required to wear black and gold shoes. The tables were to be arranged so that the males would be seated opposite their partners and children would be placed in another banqueting hall where they were to be catered for and entertained separately by entertainers and qualified childcare practitioners.

Uncle Rupert's children, grandchildren and great-grandchildren were invited and also Danny and his wife and their triplets, who were now toddlers running around. Bill and Rowna's business associates and friends had VIP invitations. The couple went all out making the venue comfortable and exclusive for their guests, ensuring that this event was to be the party of the year.

Rowna and Bill sat at the head table and welcomed their guests to begin with followed by Jovan who was the main guest speaker for the evening. A few friends and family were called upon to give speeches and that was followed by a three-course meal served by their carefully chosen reputable caterers.

The guests were encouraged to donate to the selected charity which was Rowna's orphanage in Jamaica instead of giving gifts. The family had a portrait painted of the couple to mark the occasion as memorable.

The party continued into the early hours of Sunday morning but there was no shortage of beverages and alcohol to compensate for that. The event was talked about for months afterwards because it was well planned and the day was sunny.

Chapter 29

Memories

As Bill and Rowna sat on the beach in St Lucia, they reminisced on their past when they first met in Jamaica and their journey which took them to where they were. Looking back they had built a lot of memories together. Rowna spoke about her Grandma Pearle who was a principled woman that passed on some valuable lessons, though at the time they seemed harsh but in the end worked out for her own good, and those principles were reinforced when she found her long-lost mother Annette. She also had the opportunity to learn that a broken heart can mend and provided one has ambition then 'the world is your oyster'. Looking back at her relationship with Bill, it had been a wonderful experience meeting someone who cared enough to help her make a better life than the one she previously had with her ex-husband.

She then remembered her ordeal with her cousin who took advantage of her, but she endured to the end, making sure that justice prevailed when he was imprisoned for his crime. Her dream of giving back to her community in terms of opening an orphanage came to pass and not forgetting her two gorgeous children and two grandchildren, though one died; however, she still keeps the memories of him and the relationship they had close to her heart.

These were only but a few of her blessings from God, who not only sees our faults but looks beyond and sees our needs. Rowna smiled and said to Bill, "This is a prime example of humble beginnings, but glamorous endings."

ABOUT THE AUTHOR

I am the eldest of six children and was born in Kingston, Jamaica. I attended Denham Town Primary School in Jamaica and lived in Kingston 11. I arrived in England in 1981 to join my mother and attended Brondesbury and Kilburn High School in London, then later graduated with an honours degree in finance and accounting at the Thames Valley University (Ealing Campus). I am a mother of four children, the youngest in his final year at secondary school. This is my second novel. My first was published January 2019 titled *A Journey for Perlene, jumping out of the frying pan into the fire*. I have lived in Hayes for over 22 years, but lived in Kilburn before then.